"Garnet, something tells me you and I don't punch the same holes in our precinct voting booths," Gray said.

"Since when is that a prerequisite for anything?" she asked.

"Dammed if I know."

"Gray, you swore."

"Did you think I didn't know how?" he queried.

"I wondered." She got out of the car and looked over at him. "Anything else you do that's against the rules?" She just upped the ante, like in a high-stakes poker game, and her pulse rate quickened as she waited for him to fold or call.

He came around to her side, and she could see a predatory light in his gray eyes. "Yes. I teach smart-mouthed little flirts when to shut up."

Before she could react, he pressed her against the car, framed her face with his hands, and took her mouth with swift passionate intent. . . .

WHAT ARE *LOVESWEPT* ROMANCES?

They are stories of true romance and touching emotion. We believe those two very important ingredients are constants in our highly sensual and very believable stories in the *LOVESWEPT* line. Our goal is to give you, the reader, stories of consistently high quality that may sometimes make you laugh, sometimes make you cry, but are always fresh and creative and contain many delightful surprises within their pages.

Most romance fans read an enormous number of books. Those they truly love, they keep. Others may be traded with friends and soon forgotten. We hope that each *LOVESWEPT* romance will be a treasure—a "keeper." We will always try to publish

LOVE STORIES YOU'LL NEVER FORGET
BY AUTHORS YOU'LL ALWAYS REMEMBER

The Editors

Linda Jenkins
Tall Order

BANTAM BOOKS
NEW YORK · TORONTO · LONDON · SYDNEY · AUCKLAND

TALL ORDER

A Bantam Book / May 1993

If you would be interested in receiving protective vinyl
covers for your Loveswept books, please write to this
address for information:

Loveswept
Bantam Books
P.O. Box 985
Hicksville, NY 11802

ISBN 0-553-44312-7

Published simultaneously in the United States and Canada

Bantam Books are published by Bantam Books, a division of
Bantam Doubleday Dell Publishing Group, Inc. Its trademark,
consisting of the words "Bantam Books" and the portrayal of
a rooster, is Registered in U.S. Patent and Trademark Office
and in other countries. Marca Registrada. Bantam Books,
1540 Broadway, New York, New York 10036.

PRINTED IN THE UNITED STATES OF AMERICA

OPM   0 9 8 7 6 5 4 3 2 1

One

They called him the Iceman.

During his basketball-playing days, Gray Kincaid had developed a reputation for being emotionless, for never cracking under pressure. Nerves like tempered steel, some said. He'd never understood all the hype. There was nothing special about doing what came naturally.

Gray supposed his self-control must be genetic. He couldn't recall a single instance when either of his parents had shown strong emotion. Joy, anger, grief . . . nothing shattered their quiet stoicism. And he had grown up to be just like them, perpetually calm and detached.

Tonight, however, the Iceman had been hit by a heat wave.

"Isn't she sensational? I'll bet there's not a guy in this whole place who doesn't want her."

Gray estimated there were at least fifteen thousand partying Texans jammed into the Astrohall, but he didn't bother asking which woman his friend found so desirable. He knew. "If I were a gambling man, which I'm not, you would lose."

Davis McAlpine made a rude noise, only a slight improvement over his drooling. "Don't you know beter than to con a lawyer? You haven't taken your eyes off her."

The truth annoyed Gray no end and made him defensive. "Hard to miss her, the way she flaunts all that red hair. And she's taller than just about everybody here."

"So are you." Davis's hand shot up to measure Gray's six feet six. "Clear us a path through the multitudes and I'll wangle you an introduction."

Gray had rubbed elbows, literally, with that mob for more than three hours. He wasn't crazy enough to go plunging back into it. "No, thanks. I'll pass." These days, the only crowds that interested him were the ones packing the Summit for basketball games. Flamboyant women had *never* interested him. "Not my taste."

Davis choked on his beer. "Hell's bells, Kincaid. You deserve the nickname Iceman if looking at that lady doesn't jump-start your libido."

"Who is she? Just out of curiosity," he added, careful to sound indifferent. He had no real interest in her name or anything else about her.

"You ought to try getting out in the world more, old boy. That's Garnet. Garnet Brindisi. Everyone knows her."

"No doubt." Gray's calm voice was at odds with the tight, prickly sensation crawling all over him. "Unusual name."

"She's an unusual woman." Davis took a sip, his gaze still riveted on the redhead. "What is it about her that you find so objectionable?"

"She's a flirt."

"And a damn fine one, I'd say, judging from the audience reaction."

"That's another thing," Gray said, dodging a blue-haired lady juggling two drinks and a flimsy paper plate heaped with guacamole. "She's a toucher. Has to get her hands on everybody she talks to."

"Yeah." Davis smacked his lips. "She can talk to my body anytime with those hands."

"I give up. You're a textbook case of arrested development." Gray sampled his ginger ale and silently cursed himself. After standing in a cash-bar line for twenty minutes, he ought to have had the sense to order something stronger. While he was at it, he cursed his boss for ordering Gray to represent him here.

The Houston Livestock Show and Rodeo was Bennett Townsend's favorite cause, and he had been "plumb put out" over having to miss the annual kickoff dance for volunteers. Though Gray had lived in Houston less than a year, he'd quickly learned how much delight Texans took in doing everything bigger and better.

But he'd had enough of this loud, boisterous shindig. Checking his watch, he decided he'd put in his time and could get out of there. He'd pumped the right hands and made sure the correct people knew he was standing in for Bennett. Now he looked forward to some peace and quiet, even though it meant wading through a thick stack of scouting reports.

At that instant, his eyes made contact with the redhead's. She didn't let go, and he couldn't. She smiled. The inside of his mouth turned to cotton. He tried to swallow and that didn't work. Then she started toward him, and his heartbeat felt as though it might register on the Richter scale.

The crowd parted, revealing all of her for the first

time. Now he couldn't do anything *but* swallow. Granted, she was flamboyant, a flirt, a toucher. She was also the most spectacular woman he had ever seen. That certainty hit him like an elbow in the face.

Her wine-colored walking shorts showed off a pair of stunning legs. The matching top's bright, glittery sequins reflected light as she glided through the mass of people.

He could see her eyes now, a clear, arresting brown, and he heard Davis mumble under his breath, sounding amused. That made Gray even edgier.

She homed in on him like a heat-seeking missile. Very tall, wearing very high heels, she could almost look him directly in the eye. With two fingers she stroked his tie, then brushed his lapel. "My, my, my."

Gray, who didn't believe in letting then see you sweat, started sweating as though he'd played four quarters and double overtime. He retreated a step, and kept backing up until he collided with someone behind him. The way things were going, it was probably the lady with the guacamole. "What's 'my, my, my' supposed to mean?" he demanded.

Brazen flirt that she was, she winked, advanced on him, and flicked his collar point. Her wine-tinted nail crackled against the starch. The stone in her ring, so huge and gaudy green it had to be fake, winked as boldly as she did. "You strike me as a logical thinker. See if you can figure it out for yourself."

"Games, Ms. Brindisi, are my business. Don't play them with me. I'll beat you every time."

Her eyes widened. She tossed her head and laughed, a low, throaty sound that triggered an extremely unwelcome stirring below his waist. The magnificent mane swayed; a long, wavy strand snagged on a sequin deep in her cleavage. They both stared at it for what seemed an eternity, a taut silence compounded by the savage rush of blood through his body.

At last she looked back at him, winked again, and said, "Don't bet your bloomers on it, doll. I'm a wizard at game playing. Got a lucky streak a mile wide too."

Adding "outrageous" to the list of her shortcomings, Gray leaned forward. He usually towered over people, but she stood at least six two in her sequined sandals. He still held the height advantage, not that it intimidated her.

She turned to McAlpine, her hand flitting over the splashes of chartreuse and yellow on his western-style shirt. "Davis, I swear I spotted this mess on the weather radar screen at six. Dr. Neil Frank said it means we're in for severe thunderstorms and umpteen more inches of rain."

Bending slightly, she stage-whispered, "Speaking of lots of inches, why not introduce me to your side-kick. No, wait, let me guess. His name is Mr. Gray."

Garnet saw a momentary flicker of surprise in his pale, silvery eyes before he masked it. She knew she was making an impression on the delectably tall man, albeit negative. People normally got a kick out of her cheeky banter. But the moment their eyes had locked and held, she'd sensed that this one was different.

Even from across the room, looking at him had left her a little breathless. And touching him set off a chain reaction of exciting tummy-flutters. He'd been affected too, although his body language signaled, "Keep your distance."

"Garnet Brindisi, meet Gray Kincaid."

She debated all of three seconds before offering her hand. Why waste a legitimate excuse to touch him again? Besides, she couldn't resist ruffling him a bit. He seemed like a man who valued control too much. "How about that, Gray? I guessed right."

After only a beat of hesitation, he gave her hand a firm but brief shake. One corner of his mouth lifted maybe a quarter of an inch. "The famous lucky streak, I suppose."

Fast with a comeback. She liked that. She also liked his accent, that cultured southern brand of mellow male inflection guaranteed to charm, no matter what he said. "Actually, it was more of a comment on the color of your eyes and suit." She'd be willing to wager his charcoal pin-stripe sported a Brooks Brothers label, or one equally conservative. "I assume you drive a gray car too. A Mercedes, more than likely."

"What is this, your strolling psychic routine? Part of the entertainment, like the country western band?"

"Well now, some folks think I can be downright entertaining to have around. But I'm not working tonight. Just havin' fun." As well as collecting on a very important debt. "How about you?"

"The opposite. I'm not havin' fun, but I am working."

"Shame on you, Davis," she said, reprimanding him with a rap on the arm. "Allowing this poor baby to be miserable when you're one of the official greeters. You leave me no choice except to rescue him."

After plucking up his drink and handing it to Davis, Garnet latched onto Gray's elbow and tried to propel him toward the dance floor. He didn't budge. She was used to maneuvering people around, did it all day long. But Gray Kincaid stood his ground like a granite monolith.

"Your concern is . . . touching," he said, glancing at her hand on his sleeve. "But I am not miserable and I don't need rescuing. I'm a big boy."

"Ain't it the truth?" She laid her palm on top of his neatly arranged brown hair. "Why else would I be trying to drag you onto the dance floor? Have you any idea how rare it is for a woman my size to find a man who fits?"

She sensed his withdrawal, though he didn't move. Nor could she discern any change in those cool eyes. "I'm sure for a woman like you, there's no *short*age of men."

Garnet chuckled. "You're quite clever at wordplay. I thought athletes were programmed to say 'you know' every other word, in addition to being ignorant of grammar and sentence structure."

He shoved both hands into his trouser pockets, forcing his coat open, a vaguely combative pose. "What makes you so sure I'm an athlete?"

She tore her gaze away from the leather braces that held up his pants and framed a flat stomach. "Umm, you're uncommonly tall, which I automatically associate with basketball. You're here with Davis, who works for Bennett Townsend, who owns the Wildcatters. So you must be one of his players. Simple seductive—I mean deductive—reasoning."

He was staring at her mouth, and his was open a fraction, as if he needed to breathe through it. Her heart rate speeded up. She wanted to wet her lips, but her tongue felt swollen. How extraordinary that she'd made it to twenty-six before being blindsided by a case of instant attraction. But after tonight she'd never again question what all the excitement was about.

"You're half right," Gray said, moving to create more space between them. "Bennett is my boss. I'm not one of his players. I'm the G.M."

Garnet took a deep breath, grateful that he'd maintained the thread of their conversation. "The new general manager? Goodness, am I impressed. Didn't I hear that you're the man with the golden touch? The one who's supposed to finally deliver us a title?"

His arms dropped to his sides and she detected a hint of tension in his stance. "One person can hardly ensure anything in a team sport, Ms. Brindisi. You mustn't believe everything the media tell you."

"Shucks, hon, I don't believe much of anything I hear or read. I'm what you call a freethinker."

"Why doesn't that surprise me?"

"Hey, hey, whadda ya say? Garnet and Gray. Aren't you two a colorful combination?"

They both started at the intrusion. Even without looking, Garnet recognized the culprit's grating voice. She'd grown up listening to it and his inane jokes. Ken Overton had been a neighborhood nuisance who hadn't improved with age. "Hello, Stinky."

"Keep your voice down," he hissed. "No self-respecting journalist would answer to that awful handle. Call me K.O. Get it? Like in boxing. Fits the jock image."

She had recently noticed his byline and wondered how he'd bluffed his way into a job as a sportswriter for the morning paper. "We were just discussing the media, how they tend to exaggerate and sensationalize. Did you appear to defend yourself?"

"Nope. I'm here to claim the dance you promised me earlier."

Garnet fumed, silently calling him names worse than Stinky. Naturally the little pest would have the poor timing to show up now, just when she and Gray were starting to get acquainted. "How about later, K.O.?"

"That's what you said hours ago," he whined.

So she had. Other women didn't hesitate to turn him down flat. Why did doing so cause her so much grief? Because, as Grammy had always said, she was too softhearted for her own good. If only . . .

Garnet gazed longingly at the sea of couples swaying to a mournful tune about love gone bad, then up at Gray. She trembled, overcome by an intense yearning to feel his arms around her. Just once, she wanted to be held and taken care of by someone bigger and stronger than she.

For a moment Gray looked as though he'd tapped into that need and would not allow another man to take her from him. But the moment passed and he moved away, chilling her with his rejection. Reluctantly she led Stinky toward the music, forcing herself not to turn back.

The band switched to a more upbeat song and they twirled into a Texas two-step.

"So, are you and Kincaid an item?" he inquired with his customary slyness. "I occasionally leak a bit of gossip in my column. Front page of the sports section. Great exposure."

Garnet twisted his ear, a nasty trick he'd repeatedly used on her until she had outgrown him. "If my name ever appears under your byline, Stinky, I'll scream my head off about how you came by that disgusting nickname."

"Okay, take it easy," he said, jerking his head to break her hold on his ear. "Sheesh! To think there are those who'll resort to bribery to see their name in print."

"Something tells me Mr. Kincaid isn't one of them."

"You got that right. Guy's a real enigma."

"I love a good mystery. Tell me more."

Garnet gladly endured several additional dances with her childhood nemesis in order to grill him for information about Gray.

His prep school, college, and professional achievements had been the stuff of boyhood fantasies. A scoring machine, he'd been voted onto every all-star team anybody had ever heard of. Propelled by his phenomenal shooting and record-setting defense, teams won championships, while Gray consistently earned Most Valuable Player awards.

Now he had undertaken what might turn out to be the biggest challenge of his career, that of building a title contender from the front office. The owner and local fans had been at war for years. Both factions expected Gray to turn things around. Fast.

Garnet cared nothing for those kinds of details. She wanted to know about the man. Stinky was little help in that department, saying that Gray was a notoriously private person who'd apparently had his fill of the limelight. Behind the scenes was where he preferred to operate.

She was still mulling that over when Stinky relinquished her to somebody else, who in turn yielded to yet another partner, and so on. Garnet was dimly aware of engaging in meaningless chitchat, though she paid scant attention to the subject, and even less to the men. Among all these thousands of males, only one had the ability to dominate her thoughts. Unfortunately, he had vanished.

Over her partner's shoulder she saw an acquaintance about to cut in. But in the midst of the transition a voice behind her said, "The lady is taken."

Garnet whirled around. Gray, looking quite forbidding and implacable, silently dared his would-be competitor to protest. With a discreet dip of his head, the man faded into the crowd. The music segued into a slower song, and Gray's arms engulfed her in the embrace she'd been craving.

His fingers were so long, his hand so large, that hers felt dainty by comparison. She wanted to lay her head on his shoulder and let the ballad about wasted time sweep them away. Instead, she assumed the correct dance-class position and said, "I had the feeling you'd be long gone by now."

"You and me both. But I decided to tough it out. Knowing Bennett, he'll expect a full report."

"Sounds like an assignment. Maybe you weren't kidding when you said you're working."

"I rarely kid. I'm not very good at it."

She looked up at him, luxuriating in the novelty of a taller man. "Gracious, you make life seem like such serious business."

"That's how I see it. There are so many ways it can trip you up, thrust you into situations you can't always control."

This didn't sound like the "machine" Stinky had

described, someone who had all the right moves and had known nothing but success. "That's what makes getting up in the morning interesting. The fact that we can't predict what's going to happen every minute."

"There are times when I'd sell my soul for predict-ability. It would sure make my job easier."

Her hand rested lightly on his shoulder where she felt a muscle tighten. Prompted by an instinct to soothe him, she started to knead with her thumb. She caught herself and stopped. "Speaking of jobs, what's your committee assignment?"

For a few seconds he looked as if he didn't com-prehend the question. "Oh, you mean as a volunteer. I'm not one."

"Since you're here at Bennett's command, I won't blow the whistle on you for gate-crashing. Of course, we could legalize your presence by signing you up."

"Bennett's tried to recruit me. So far I've been able to put him off." He gazed out over the crowd and shook his head. "I'm not much for parties or country music or beer and smoke."

Garnet pursed her lips, then grinned. Gray needed educating, and that's what she did best. "Volunteers deserve to kick up their heels once a year. This dance is small compensation for all the hours these people donate."

"What is it they actually do?"

"I could give you a list, but your eyes would glaze over before I got halfway through. Bear in mind that it takes seventy-two committees and nearly ten thou-sand people to cover everything from agricultural education to western art."

"And it's all done by volunteers?"

Either she'd gotten him sincerely interested, or he was a fine actor. "Put it this way, if you had a million and a half people coming to visit in the next two weeks, you couldn't afford to pay for enough help to entertain and take care of them."

She barely noticed his misstep. "I didn't realize it was such a big deal. I admit I'm guilty of tuning Bennett out when he gets carried away with the Rodeo."

"Then it's time you started listening. Most of us do this because we enjoy it, but we definitely aren't in it for fun. All of us are involved because we're committed to the Rodeo's purposes."

"Which are?"

"Scholarships, endowments, and research projects." Garnet could have gone on forever; she was a tireless promoter of education. Tonight, however, she'd discovered a more compelling priority in Gray Kincaid.

Her luck had prevailed and she'd ended up in his arms. She wasn't about to spoil that by sounding preachy.

"There you are at last, darlin'. Been looking for you all night."

Bouncing up next to them, doing their version of what Garnet described as the pump-handle swing, were her late grandparents' dearest friends. "Hey, Dewdaddy. How you doing, Mrs.?"

"I'll be right as rain, dearie, if I can get old Dew to sit out the next one. His style of dancing is more exhausting than my aerobics-for-grannies class."

Garnet performed introductions, and while Mrs. studied Gray with a speculative twinkle in her eyes,

Dewey Whitt dug in the breast pocket of his cream-colored western suit.

"Got something to give you." He passed her a long envelope with his company's letterhead on it. "Hoo-wee! You were surely on a roll last night. Thought you were gonna wipe me out completely 'fore I could get away."

She tapped his shoulder twice with the envelope. "I'm good, but not that good. You're just extra generous."

Smiling, she recalled that, as usual, his final wager had sweetened the pot. Garnet suspected that he proposed the winner take all hands because he knew the money was vital to her and he could well afford to lose it.

"Aw, I'm no match for a young 'un like you. But that don't stop me from trying. Maybe next time I'll get lucky." With that, he jacked up his wife's arm and they went seesawing away.

Having no place to stow it, she shuffled and fussed with the envelope. The small sequined purse clipped to her belt had room for only a lipstick, keys, and several folded bills. Finally Gray snatched it from her and crammed it into his coat pocket.

Garnet looked into his eyes. She saw a flash of something fierce. Then they went blank. How did he do that? And why was he clutching her so tightly when minutes ago he'd been determined to keep her at arm's length? His only comment was, "Dewdaddy?"

"When their daughter first started to talk, she kept getting confused about whether she should call him Dewey or Daddy. She finally settled on a combination, and it stuck."

"I see."

Garnet tried to relax in his embrace, but every inch of him was as tightly drawn as a new wire fence. She waited for further questions or observations on the Whitts, but he said nothing. Out of desperation, she asked, "How about it? Have I convinced you to enlist as a volunteer?"

She held her breath, hoping his prolonged silence meant he was weakening. Then she asked herself why she'd made it her mission to convert him. Perhaps she was seeking some assurance she'd see him again, though his becoming a volunteer would not guarantee that.

"I will give you the same answer I've given Bennett. I'll think about it."

"Fair enough," she said, feeling reckless enough to try pinning him down, yet too wary to push him at this point.

Gray kept her on the floor for two more dances, each tune progressively slower as the band worked toward the finale. They didn't speak, but she was intensely aware of everything about him. The graceful play of his athlete's body, the tantalizing man-smell of him, the slight abrasion of a day's beard against her temple, the warmth of his breath as it ruffled her hair. She wanted to soak up each sensation, to never let go.

Inevitably the music stopped, and for the merest second he continued to hold her. When he did release her, she felt bereft and unreasonably disappointed. An usual, she covered up with folksy humor. "Well, as my Uncle Bud would say, 'There ain't nothing left to do but fight or go home.' "

He didn't smile. "Where are you parked?"

A spark of hope kindled. "By the Astroarena. Why?"

"I'll see you to your car."

"You don't have to bother." *Please bother.* "I came by myself and I can leave by myself. I'm used to it."

She didn't mistake his brief skeptical look. "Haven't you been listening to the news lately? Crime is rampant in Houston. Lone women should avoid parking lots at night."

"Every female I know pays attention to that. But I don't think there's any danger here. Not with all these people pouring out at the same time."

"I'll see you to your car," he repeated, his hand insistent on her elbow.

"Who said chivalry is dead?" She could tease even as a delicious tingle skittered up her spine.

"This has nothing to do with chivalry." His grip got stronger and he spoke through gritted teeth. "It's just common sense."

He retained his hold while they battled the swarm of people so she could reclaim her trenchcoat and umbrella. When they stepped outside, it was raining, as it had been nearly every day since the first of January. Like a perfect gentleman, he took the umbrella, raised it one-handed, and placed his other hand at her waist.

Garnet had arrived early and the trek to her car didn't take long. Faced with leaving when she didn't want to, she grinned up at Gray and blurted out the first thing that popped into her head.

"Well, here we are. You've walked me to my door. Is this where you kiss me good night?"

Two

I ought to do just that! Crush her against me and kiss the sass right out of her. He wanted to—badly—and she'd been asking for it all evening, flirting, touching, making promises with those sexy, pouty lips.

Reminding himself that he wasn't a man who gave in to dangerous urges, Gray took the keys and unlocked her car. The Cadillac was as long as Cleopatra's barge and gaudy green, like her ring.

"Call me old-fashioned, but it takes more than a few dances for me to decide if I want to kiss a lady."

"Oh, I do like a man who's selective." Was she agreeing or goading him? "Don't pay any attention to me. I sometimes shoot off my mouth without thinking. Forget I even brought up the subject of a kiss."

Goading, he decided. Doing a nice job of it too. "I promise not to give it another thought."

Flinging open the huge door, she laughed, a seductive, low-pitched sound that again caused his body to override his brain. She arranged herself in the seat, hit the starter, and said, "You've been such a perfect gentleman. I wouldn't be able to sleep a wink for worrying about you getting wet.

Keep the umbrella. It's more your color than mine, anyway."

Before he could protest, she yanked the massive door shut and roared off. He should have guessed she'd be the type to drive a garish, attention-getting, twenty-year-old convertible.

Gray was positive he heard her yell "Yee-haw!" but that was probably because he'd been hearing it all evening. He had no idea what the term meant, just that Texans shouted it like a battle cry.

He stood there a few seconds, clutching the dinky parasol with both hands while he watched her car dart and weave its way toward the Kirby Drive exit. Finally, he gave his head a rueful shake and started slogging through the standing water.

By the time he reached his gray Mercedes, he was thoroughly soaked, thoroughly out of sorts, and, rational or not, he blamed Garnet and her pushy ways. If not for her, he'd be snug and dry at home, taking care of business.

Kincaids were famous for keeping themselves and their lives under strict control, and until now, Gray had easily followed suit. But this first season of his new job was consuming almost every waking hour, and it hadn't fallen into place as readily as most things he'd attempted. He had no time for a woman of any sort, certainly not one as troublesome and unsettling as Garnet Brindisi.

He tipped the umbrella to shake off the excess water, then groaned. He'd crossed the parking lot huddled beneath a baby-pink umbrella decorated with plump, gray flying Dumbos. "Damnable redhead."

Gray was still experimenting with names to call her when he woke the next morning. It was raining. Again. His mood was as dark and foul as the weather outside. He hadn't slept well, nor had he made any headway on his homework. All because of the woman and the incriminating envelope that lay on his nightstand like a live grenade.

He had not meant to look inside. No way. But, hell, it hadn't been sealed and the flap had peeled back when he'd removed it from his damp coat last night. It was impossible not to see the money. Hundred dollar bills. Ten of them.

He couldn't think of a legitimate reason why the old man would be giving Garnet that much cash. His imagination did come up with a sordid possibility or two. That wouldn't wash either. The guy's wife had doted on Garnet.

Stomach churning, Gray rolled out of bed. He hated to contemplate what game she might be playing, hated caring enough to wonder. Yet something within him clamored to know more about her. As he searched for the phone book, it occurred to him that his ordered existence had taken on soap opera overtones.

Less than thirty minutes later, he wheeled into the driveway of a red brick bungalow. He'd found only one Brindisi listed—Garnet. Gray didn't believe there would be two of them, but neither could he picture the woman he'd met living in a neighborhood of modest, well-maintained homes. This was a family setting. He didn't see it as the sort of place she'd fit in.

Although it was barely eight o'clock on Saturday

morning, light shone through the gleaming panes of a leaded glass door. The glow looked cheerful and welcoming on a sodden, dreary day like this one. No harm in checking it out.

He scooped up the umbrella and envelope. The rain continued its steady torrent and he took giant steps to reach the sheltered doorway. He hesitated only a second before hitting the button.

The door opened. Face to face with her, the image of Garnet as a kept woman, commanding a cool grand for a night of hot sex, struck him as so absurd, so implausible, he laughed aloud.

She snapped her fingers. "I have it. You're delirious because you have decided to become a Rodeo volunteer and couldn't wait to tell me the good news."

"No, I—" He had to stop and choke back another burst of laughter. "Not exactly." He wasn't ready to admit that volunteering had crossed his mind during the night.

"I'd hate to think you're so rude you would guffaw at my gardening outfit."

"In case you haven't noticed, it's pouring. Not very good gardening weather."

"Which is why I'm dressed this way."

She had on a mustard yellow vinyl slicker, the kind little kids wore to go puddle stomping. Perched atop her red hair sat a Donald Duck cap, its orange beak extending out over her brow. On her feet were rubber boots the color of frog skin, complete with bulging gold and black eyes and red soles that resembled a grinning Kermit mouth.

"Would you like to come in?"

That, and more. Her unpainted lips looked very tempting, and oddly enough, the desire to kiss her was far stronger than it had been last night. She had that effect on him. "I, uh, stopped by to return these."

"Oh," she breathed, removing the items from his hand. She propped the umbrella in a corner and gazed at the crumpled envelope, frowning slightly. "You must have had me discombobulated, Gray Kincaid. I can't believe I forgot something this important."

He waited, hoping, dreading that she would elaborate. When she said nothing, he didn't know whether to feel disappointed or relieved. He'd still like an explanation for why Dewey Whitt had given her a thousand bucks, but could think of no reason why he deserved one. Basically he just wanted to be with her for a while, and that was the thing that concerned him most of all.

"Let's get you out of the damp," she said, tugging on the sleeve of his red-and-white team warm-up jacket.

He followed her into a family room furnished with an overstuffed couch and chairs covered in bright prints. Unlike the museumlike house he'd grown up in, unlike his present home, this one was warm and cozy with just enough clutter to make it look comfortable. Gray inhaled the yeasty smell of baking. His mouth watered and his stomach growled.

Garnet continued into the kitchen. He trailed along and she gestured for him to sit in one of the four padded chairs. She whisked off her headgear and plunked it on the round table. "If you're willing to wait ten minutes, you can sample some homemade cinnamon rolls."

"Are we alone?" he blurted out. "I mean, does anyone else live here? With you?"

If she recognized his obvious ploy, she overlooked it. "The house belonged to my grandmother Tyler and I spent most of my growing-up time here. Grammy died four years ago and left it to me. I've lived alone since."

The picture still didn't jibe. He'd been so sure she would live in a singles complex, surrounded by hard-edged contemporary furniture.

He watched her peel off the slicker. Underneath she wore a white T-shirt that sported a green iguana crawling from the breast pocket. His fingers flexed. He wanted to touch her, fit his palm over the iguana and . . .

"If it weren't for the trees, I could see your house from my high-rise." He hadn't aimed to let that slip, but he was desperate to get his mind on anything besides the front of her T-shirt. When he had looked up her address in his Key Map, he'd been shocked to see that the Southwest Freeway was about the only thing separating them.

"You must be in Greenway," she mused, opening the refrigerator. Removing a container, she gave it a couple of vigorous shakes. "High-rise, high price."

That sounded like criticism. He shrugged. "The only reason I chose there is it's close to work. I can walk."

"To the Summit?"

"Yes. Lots of days I never venture beyond a square-block radius."

"You need to get out more," she said, echoing Davis's suggestion. "Person's apt to calcify in such a narrow environment. Houston has loads of fun things to do."

No doubt she had tried every one. "Maybe I'll have more time to explore in the off-season. With any luck, that won't be until June." If he had to take the court himself, he was determined the team would make it to the playoffs.

She reached for two glasses on the top shelf of a cabinet. The stretch gave him a whole new appreciation of how faded jeans could flatter the female form. She turned, holding the glasses at shoulder height. "I don't see you as the type who puts much faith in luck."

Sometimes she had uncanny insight into his character. That disturbed him. "You're right. My first coach taught us that luck is spelled W-O-R-K."

"I, of course, beg to differ." With a flourish she filled both glasses and placed one in front of him. With the other, she toasted, "Here's to luck."

"Ah, yes. The famous lucky streak again."

"Wait and see if I'm not right in the end." Mischief lighted her eyes and almost disguised the cryptic advice. "Now drink your juice. And try not to have any accidents."

"Yes, Mommy."

● ● ●

Garnet rinsed off their sticky plates and reflected on her earlier faux pas. Kindergarten-age youngsters frequently needed mothering in addition to teaching. She was so accustomed to performing the dual roles that she sometimes blundered and treated the wrong people as she did her five-year-olds.

Gray Kincaid didn't need mothering, nor did she feel the least bit maternal toward him. But he'd responded to her slip with good humor, had even smiled before answering with feigned obedience.

He seemed like a different man this morning, more open and approachable. They might call him the Iceman, and he definitely appeared that way on the surface. But she didn't necessarily accept that his calm went all the way through.

Maybe the rolls had done it, she thought, smiling to herself. One of Grammy's favorite sayings had been that a girl could win a man with the smell of perfume, but she couldn't keep him without the smell of food. Archaic by today's standards, Garnet admitted. Yet she'd never seen a man, or anyone for that matter, who didn't appreciate home cooking. She could tell her baking had surprised him. But he hadn't let that stop him from asking for seconds.

"Quite a backyard you have," he commented, interrupting her thoughts. He was standing at the French doors that led to the patio. "Looks like a formal garden."

She spun around and beamed at him. He couldn't have paid her a higher compliment. "I think I'm a farmer at heart. I love to grow things, especially flowers. They're like children. Lavish them with time and attention and they'll bloom for you."

"You have a talent for it, all right." Thunder rumbled just as he opened the door.

"To me, digging in the dirt is more therapeutic than psychiatry, and a heck of a lot cheaper." She glanced at the clock before donning her slicker and hat and following him onto the covered patio. Her frog boots squeaked on the flagstone.

"You've apparently done plenty of digging."

"Not as much this year as usual because of the rain. I kept waiting for a dry weekend to plant my jonquils, but they can't be put off any longer."

"Jonquils care when they go in the ground?"

"For everything there is a season. Don't you remember your Ecclesiastes? A time to plant, and a time to pluck up what is planted."

His brows lifted, probably because he hadn't antici-pated her quoting the Bible. She didn't take offense. "You don't mind diving into all that mud?"

"Heck, no, sweetie. I'll just pretend I'm six again, making mudpies in my playhouse." She slipped on some rubber gloves, picked up a bag of bonemeal, and brandished her bulb planter like a cutlass.

He strolled to the edge of the patio, still beneath the overhang, though barely. "Need any help?"

"Don't even consider it. I refuse to be responsible for you ruining those lily-white hightops." She gave his outfit a quick once-over. He was clearly dressed for basketball. "I thought you said you don't play anymore."

"No. I said I'm not one of Bennett's players. But I still hit the court as often as possible. Helps to keep my reflexes sharp. Good for staying in shape too."

She'd second that! "Can't take the player out of the boy, eh?"

"Something like that." He crossed his arms and leaned against one of the patio columns.

How could such cool intent in those gray eyes make her so hot? She examined a bulb with exaggerated interest, then jabbed the planter in the ground. "You're playing this morning?"

"Getting in some practice." He paused a second before adding, "It's All-Star weekend. The big game is tomorrow. This afternoon I'll be playing in a shortened version for old-timers."

Garnet propped the backs of her hands on her hips and gazed up at him. "You don't look much like an old-timer. Are you sure that's what they call it?"

"Actually, it's billed as the Legends game, but I feel a little presumptuous applying that term to myself."

"I don't see why. Stinky called you a legend." He'd also told her that Gray had the softest pair of hands ever to play the game. Whatever that meant, he'd said it with such reverence, she assumed it must be exceptional. Personally, she hadn't found his hands soft at all, and she had been very aware of them while they were dancing.

"Like a lot of sportswriters, your pal Stinky isn't

above embellishing for the sake of a story. He was probably trying to impress you with statistics."

"Ken Overton grew up three doors down, and I've known him since first grade. He learned quite a while back that he's not likely to impress me. Besides, my brother's the one who stuck him with the nickname Stinky."

"With good reason, I assume."

"You better believe it." Garnet watched him chase an ornamental pebble with the toe of his shoes. She knew Gray was psyching himself up to say something that didn't come easy. Body language had been part of one of the counseling courses she had taken in graduate school.

Sometimes it was best to confront; other times, best to wait. She waited.

He hooked his thumbs in the pockets of his red warm-up jacket and focused on the azalea bed alongside the garage. "Do you know anything about basketball?"

Why was that so hard to ask? "My brother played when he went to Lamar, but turned down a scholarship to UT. Typical of Ty to act so perverse."

Gray outlined his watch, squinted at the dripping redbud, toyed with a leaf on the blooming sweet olive. "I have some tickets. To the games. Today and tomorrow."

A ripple of excitement settled in her stomach. Garnet crossed her fingers and willed herself to keep quiet. This might turn out better than she'd dared to hope.

"The game starts at three. I can leave a ticket in your name at the Summit box office if you're interested."

"I'm interested."

He shifted, feet wide apart, hands behind him, like a soldier at parade rest. For some reason, he was having difficulty looking at her. "I have extras. If there's someone you'd like to bring."

She bit back a grin. Could it be that the Iceman had thawed enough to probe subtly to find out if she was involved with anybody? "One ticket is fine. Thank you."

"You're welcome."

Bless his heart. He was so ill at ease, he'd reverted to excessive politeness. "I have a couple of prior commitments I have to honor, but I'll try to rush and get there in time for the tipoff."

"Oh," was all he said, giving her nary a clue as to whether he was pleased or disappointed by her acceptance.

"Maybe I'll see you there?" She asked because his invitation had been frustratingly noncommittal.

He studied her for quite a while, as if waging an internal debate. At last he nodded. "Maybe."

Garnet blew out a gust of air as she watched him open the gate and disappear down the driveway. When she heard his car start, she went back to her planting with the strangest inkling that Gray had come here for some reason other than to return the envelope and her umbrella. She'd also lay odds that inviting her to the game had not been on his agenda.

The possibility that he had succumbed to impulse was so heartening that she began to whistle a tune about dancing daisies. Maybe there was hope for him. And her.

She made quick work of the ten dozen jonquils, then draped her muddy gear over a patio chaise. Once inside, she took only a minute to scrub her hands before grabbing the phone and punching out a familiar number.

"Carol, hi. It's Garnet. Sorry to call so early on Saturday, but I'm on a tight schedule today. Is it okay if I drop by in about half an hour? I have something to give you, something beautiful and green."

"Don't tell me," Carol said sardonically. "You've been at the poker table again and poor Mr. Whitt's wallet is a few ounces lighter this morning."

Garnet smiled at her friend's accusation. "You know me so well. But don't waste any sympathy on Dewdaddy and his cronies. All of them can well afford the losses, and besides, they accept the fact that I'm fleecing them for a good cause."

"I suppose." Like all good CPAs, Carol took any loss of money personally. "The few people I've known who won at gambling either rushed out and bought a new car or jetted off to Europe."

"Land sakes, dear heart, why would I want a new car? It took me a month of Sundays to find the perfect one to start with. I'm keeping it forever." Garnet shook her head. "As for Europe, I'd seen all I needed to by the time I was six." Though there was no doubt the continent would present a different picture to her twenty years later, she still had no desire to go back.

"Don't think I'm complaining about how you spend the bounty. I'm just glad you share our objectives. After all, your generosity made it possible for us to award several extra scholarships last year."

"Which is only fair. The group gave me a helping hand when I needed it. Now I'm trying to give something back."

"You've done more than your part." Carol let out an audible sigh. "Even if a few of the more conservative members grumble about 'ill-gotten gains.'"

"I'm sorry they don't approve. But I believe in our mission too strongly to let moral indignation stop me. I don't lie, cheat, or steal to get the money and that makes it respectable enough in my book."

"Hey, I'm on the same bandwagon as you, remember? Every girl we can help to get an education is one more woman who can take care of herself."

Eight years earlier, when Garnet applied for one of the scholarships given by a local businesswomen's organization, Carol had interviewed her. The older woman, owner of a successful accounting firm, became inspiration, mentor, and finally, friend. "Yes, and both of us are good examples that it works."

"Thanks to you, it's working better than ever. Stop by anytime. I'll be here."

After hanging up, Garnet pondered her reflection in the dressing-table mirror. Even Carol, herself a scholarship recipient, had no idea how much satisfaction Garnet got from providing girls with an opportunity to get a college degree.

She was totally devoted to education. That was the real reason she'd become a Rodeo volunteer. The two million dollars they'd present this year, as scholarships and research grants, was an all-time record.

But it was much more gratifying to see the results on a personal level. Which was why she repeatedly chaired the group's education committee. She enjoyed meeting the applicants and their families, got a thrill from listening to them talk about their aspirations. And she had experienced an almost maternal fulfillment when the first young woman she'd sponsored invited her to graduation.

Every woman needed the assurance that she could function independently. Garnet had vowed never to be like her mother, subject to a man's whims, drifting around the globe with no place to call home.

While Lucky Brindisi hadn't been much of a father in the traditional sense, he had always let her know that she could be anything she wanted. For that alone, she loved him.

But she'd known better than to rely on him to pay for her college education. It had become a matter of pride that she be able to get her degree without parental assistance. She'd chosen a smallish state university because tuition was lower, and armed with two scholarships plus a night job in a 24-hour truck stop, she'd not only made it through, but graduated with honors.

Nearly everybody had questioned her decision to become a teacher except Lucky and Grammy. Garnet chuckled. That was about the only subject those two had ever agreed on.

She rose and headed for the shower. Would Gray be surprised to learn she was a kindergarten teacher? Probably, provided he worked up enough interest to find out. That was the wild card.

He was a classic close-to-the-vest player, but she had more than luck in her favor. She was a master at reading people. He might present more resistance, more of a challenge than most, but Garnet relished a challenge.

It was five minutes before three when Garnet sprinted into the Summit. She hadn't realized Humble was quite a distance away, and then the den of Cub Scouts she'd presented the program to were exceptionally curious. They'd asked tons of questions, all of which she answered patiently. The delay made swinging by home to change clothes impossible.

Panting, she rushed to the box office, claimed her ticket, and took off to find the seat. "Hey, Tex," a man said, as he fell into step beside her and tipped an imaginary hat. "Where's your horse?"

Garnet grinned, but didn't slow her pace. "Tied to the hitchin' post out front, pardner." Drawing attention was nothing new to her. She attributed it to her height and the unusual color and abundance of her hair.

Today, duded up in her authentic working cowboy attire, she stood out like a giraffe at a tea dance. Gray would be appalled. On the other hand, getting him to notice her was half the battle. As Aunt Blanche used to say, "First you stun 'em, then you rope 'em." This getup ought to stun him good.

Her seat was in the third row, and she collapsed in it just in time to rise again for the national anthem. Player introductions followed. Among the cluster of tall men clad in a spectrum of colors, Garnet thought she spotted Gray's back. No one else inspired that peculiar little inner tingling. But, as a starting guard, his name wasn't announced until last.

He moved to the sidelines, his walk a lithe blend of strength and grace unique to athletes. For a heart-stopping moment his eyes met hers. His gaze burned into her like a laser. Then, with a swift jerk of both hands, he ripped off his warm-up pants.

Garnet's breath rushed out with a whoosh. Warmth bathed her body, made her squirm in the seat. Her clothes felt too heavy and confining. She heard herself whimper.

Stripping down like that was unbearably sexy. And he'd held her gaze while doing it, very deliberately, as if he were performing an intimate act for her eyes only.

"Not sure if you want to kiss me, huh?" she said softly. "Ten to one, you'll soon eat those words."

Three

At the final buzzer, Gray traded handshakes, back slaps, and congratulations with his teammates. It felt good being in uniform again. Winning felt better. He'd retired only five years ago, after his best season ever. Nobody had understood why he opted to quit at the peak of his career. The only explanation he'd given was that he was ready to try winning from the bench.

He had enjoyed coaching, had proven to himself he could succeed at it, but his ultimate ambition had always been a general manager's position. Lately, though, he'd started to question his game plan. Since last night, he'd been questioning his sanity.

He wasn't the type to get distracted by a woman, especially one he'd just met. And if he were in the market for that sort of distraction, he'd never choose a siren like Garnet Brindisi.

Finally he allowed himself to look at the third row. It had been a real endurance test to keep his eyes and his mind on the court. The back of his neck had itched with the certainty that Garnet was watching him. On the floor, at least, his technique hadn't suffered. Nothing surpassed the sense of control that playing gave him.

She had a crowd gathered around her. What else is new? Gray thought irritably. Her bizarre outfit seemed to be the topic of conversation. Had she dressed normally, perish the thought, the end result would have been the same. She simply radiated the kind of energy that lured people.

Unlike last night, her circle of admirers consisted primarily of kids. There were more than a few of the grown-up male variety as well. Reluctant to join the pack, he hovered on the fringe and listened.

"I've told you that most everything a cowboy owned served more than one purpose." She pulled a red bandanna from her back pocket and held it out to a little girl. "What would you use this for?"

The girl folded it into a triangle and held it up like a mask. "Excellent," Garnet praised. "Tied in place, that will keep dust out of your nose and mouth." She then rearranged the cloth to cover her model's ears. "In the winter they used it for added warmth."

A flick of her wrist and she was dipping the bandanna in an imaginary stream and wringing it out. "To beat the summer heat, they'd wet this and tie it on their heads. It could also take the place of a sweatband and, in extreme emergencies, surprise! Use it to blow your nose."

She was so engrossed in the act she might well have been performing Shakespeare. Her audience was wide-eyed and equally absorbed. They dutifully contributed ideas about the versatility of a cowboy hat, from hauling water to put out a campfire to shading the face while taking a nap.

Then she pointed at Gray, diverting all eyes in his direction. "Behold, the Iceman cometh." She marched over to stand in front of him. "Let's see if he can think of a reason why the hat has this neck cord."

"I'm thinking of a noose," he replied blandly.

She giggled. "Very clever. But no, they called it a kissing cord. Suppose a cowboy had been on a trail drive for months. When he got back to town, he might like to kiss a pretty girl." She thumbed off the black felt and let it hang down her back. "This way he didn't lose his hat and still had his hands free."

Not for the first time, he contemplated kissing her smart mouth, and maybe a few other things while he was at it. Gray knew she went out of her way to needle him every chance she got. Except this morning at her house, when she'd played the role of hostess, he had relaxed and gotten comfortable, totally surprising himself. That was the trouble, a man never could be sure he had her pegged.

"Can't resist putting on a show, can you?" He had an unnatural urge to needle her back.

"Just a teaser," she replied, unfazed. "I've already done my two performances for today." Her hand burrowed inside a beat-up leather satchel and came out with a stack of business cards. "Any of you buckaroos want to learn all about the legend of the cowboy, tell your teacher, or your scout leader, or your parents. They can call that number and get you a program scheduled."

She smiled and patted heads and answered more questions. "Remember, rodeos began as contests between working cowboys. If you come out to the Astrodome, most of the events you see will be the same ones they started back in the eighteen hundreds."

Gray was hot and sweaty, needed a shower, yet he stayed. "What was all that about?" he asked when the crowd broke up and drifted away.

"You know me. Always on the lookout to stir up a little interest in the Rodeo."

"By masquerading as a cowboy?" Didn't she own even one piece of conventional clothing?

She took off her black hat and slapped it against her thigh, as if it were dusty from the trail. "I'll tell ya, Pil-grim," she said, shifting to a terrible John Wayne imitation, "these duds are the genuine article."

"Uh-huh. Is that your volunteer job, to go around as a walking advertisement for the Rodeo?"

"Talking, actually." She peeled back her leather vest to reveal a small bronze megaphone pinned to the pocket of her blue-and-white gingham shirt.

"Big Mouth Award," he read, rubbing the letters. When his finger rose with the deep intake of her breath, he snatched it back. Damn! Why had he touched her *there*?

"I, um . . ." Her voice caught, sounded breathless. She wet her lips and began again. "I'm a member of the Speakers Committee. We give speeches to groups about different aspects of the Rodeo. I chose the cowboy legend because I prefer to work with children, and they really enjoy the visual effects."

To his dismay, Gray was enjoying them too. Garnet in spurs and leather chaps presented interesting possibilities. He forced them out of his mind. He wasn't the kinky type. "Why didn't you tell me this morning that you had to be somewhere? I wouldn't have wasted so much of your time."

"You didn't waste my time. I was glad you showed up. Did I thank you for returning my things?"

"More than once." The cash in that cursed envelope

had started to obsess him. Telling himself it didn't concern him hadn't dampened his curiosity.

"So, did you have a gaggle of groupies hanging around when you were a big-time star? Looking for a piece of the action, so to speak?"

Gray felt a flush creep up his neck. He knew he should have made straight for the locker room. "Why would you think that?"

"Sports figures are today's heroes. When they look like you, it stands to reason you'd be a prime target."

"I was engaged during the time I was a player. There was no need to mess around with groupies."

A little frown formed as she digested that news. "You were engaged for eight years?"

"More or less," he mumbled, frustrated at how easily she'd dragged out the confession. The engagement had been official for only two of those years. For much longer than that, he and Susannah and both their families had taken for granted that they would someday marry.

"That was one patient woman."

"Yes, she was." It still bothered Gray to remember the relief he had felt when Susannah eventually decided to call it off. Failure never set well with him, especially when he had to accept most of the blame for it. It was sobering to have someone he'd known his whole life accuse him of being dispassionate, incapable of a deep emotional commitment to anyone. But he hadn't denied her accusation, nor had he tried to change her mind.

Garnet's teeth worked on her lower lip. The frown

deepened. Uncharacteristically, she avoided meeting his gaze. Under her breath she murmured something that sounded like "luck when you need it." She looked ready to bolt. "I'm sorry. I shouldn't detain you any longer. Thank you for the ticket."

The words were jerky and forced, and her posture rigid. Why the sudden change? Within seconds she'd gone from teasing him to sounding as proper as Miss Manners. When Garnet's animation faded, he felt the loss. Her vitality was energizing. Addictive.

"There are a few questions I want to ask you," he said, seizing on the one sure means of reviving her enthusiasm. "Regarding the Rodeo. How about tonight, over dinner?"

She picked up the satchel and slid the straps onto her shoulder. "I don't think that's a very good idea."

The brush-off angered him. "Correct me if I'm wrong, but last night I got the impression, a rather strong one in fact, that you would welcome my attention."

"That was last night, before you told me you're old-fashioned. Well, mister, so am I." She jabbed her index finger in the middle of his number 50. "Which means I don't mess around with another woman's man."

The missing puzzle piece fell into place. "The engagement ended, but not in marriage. No fiancée, no wife, no other woman, period."

Her brows rose into perfectly matched peaks and her mouth shaped a silent O. Her smile dazzled him. "In that case, dinner sounds perfect. Shall I dress?"

"Please." His voice croaked, like that of an adolescent hit hard by puberty. "We'll be going to a dinner that's part of the All-Star activities. I guess you'd call it semi-dressy." Since he hadn't taken a date more than a couple of times, he couldn't recall what the women wore.

"Gosh, I'd better rush home and polish up my tiara." She laughed heartily at his stricken look. "Just kidding."

"I'll pick you up at seven." Gray headed for the locker room, wondering where all this was leading, and afraid he knew. Every time he got close to her, he ended up issuing another unplanned invitation.

"Say, Iceman?" He halted and glanced over his shoulder. "You have great moves for an old-timer." She winked. "Great legs too."

He rolled his eyes at her impertinence and forced himself to stroll nonchalantly into the tunnel. Internally, he fought the childish urge to leap up and do a high-five.

Garnet deplored tardiness. As a result she usually overcompensated by being early. Tonight she'd taken it to the extreme. She was ready and Gray wasn't due for forty-five minutes. If she sat down, her silk skirt would be a mess of wrinkles. On the other hand, standing up until he got there would be dumb. So would undressing. Dithering over it was dumber still.

Like many of her personal quirks, the punctuality fetish could be traced to her father. Unless Lucky Brindisi had a card game scheduled, he had no concept of time. Her mother always laughed it off, saying, "That's my Lucky."

Anna had made a career of being patient and tolerant, indulging, even encouraging Lucky to do exactly as he pleased. Garnet could not fathom such blind devotion. But long ago she'd had to accept that her parents' lives and priorities bore little relation to her own. They had each other, and had managed to make their honeymoon last for over thirty years.

While her brother Ty had turned inward and become very self-contained, Garnet had opened herself to their grandmother. For years Maggie Tyler had been the constant in her life. Grammy had taught her so much. How Garnet wished she could ask her advice now.

Humming, she waltzed over to the white-framed cheval mirror and pirouetted to check her hemline. Fashionably but not scandalously short. The plum-colored outfit was far from her flashiest, but neither was it conservative. Clearly, Gray had typecast her as flaky and flippant. So she couldn't wear something modest and demure, giving him the idea that she would change her style to suit him. He had to learn that things are not always what they seem.

A tall order, that one. In every way. She knew he wouldn't react well to being pursued, but that didn't mean she couldn't intrigue him until he decided to do the pursuing himself.

To pass the time until seven, she leaned on the kitchen island and sorted a stack of kindergarten artwork. Each Monday morning, before the class arrived, she put up a new bulletin board display. Next week's theme would be the solar system. They'd gone on a field trip to the planetarium, and several of her students had water-colored some pretty amazing versions of what they'd seen.

When the doorbell rang, she shuffled the papers into her briefcase and hurried to the entry hall, where the banjo clock was chiming the three-quarter hour.

"I'm early," he said when she opened the door.

"You're early," she said at the same time, inordinately pleased by his promptness. It seemed like a good omen.

Touching the damp sleeve of his black overcoat, she drew him into the small foyer. "If it doesn't stop raining soon, we're all going to start mildewing."

"Um." For a few seconds he silently took in every detail of her shimmering multicolored brocade jacket and sarong skirt. He gave more than passing interest to the metallic braidwork that bordered the neckline and hem and covered the buttons.

Garnet endured his scrutiny with a confident smile, though her heart drummed like a crazed bongo player. When she could no longer stand it, she asked, "Do you approve?"

"Oh yeah."

His voice was low, and very tight. It conjured up visions of lighting a fire, snuggling on the couch, and letting nature take its course. Instead, she asked, "Do we have time for a glass of wine? I can offer you a very fine vintage-September."

"My favorite," he said with the merest hint of a smile, then shrugged out of his coat and hung it on the hall tree. "Lead on."

The heels of her black evening sandals pattered over the wood floor of the living and dining rooms.

She heard Gray's muffled footsteps right behind her. It was so strange, her desperately wanting him to be here, yet being tied in knots because he was.

She pulled a bottle from the wine rack, checked the label, and nodded once. "This was a gift. I had no idea whether it was worth drinking or not, so I took it to the wine guy at my grocery store."

"And he thought it was worth drinking."

"Better than that. He said serve it to company, providing the menu didn't feature cheeseburgers on the grill."

Gray appropriated the bottle and corkscrew and went to work. He accomplished the task efficiently, as though he did it for a living. To Garnet, extracting corks without fuss was a singularly masculine trait. Not that Gray needed extra points in that department.

He poured a small amount for each of them to sample. She sipped, gulped, screwed up her face. "This is so embarrassing, and it happens to me all the time. I'm supposed to gush reverently, about bouquet or body or some such. In reality, I think this tastes worse than cough medicine. My palate is way too unsophisticated to appreciate the subtleties here."

Gray took a swallow. He shook his head and shuddered. "You're right. Tastes vile to me too."

Garnet clinked her glass against his. "A toast, then. To three-ninety-eight red and fair weather ahead."

They both laughed, set down their glasses, and prepared to brave yet another thunderstorm.

• • •

When Garnet and Gray arrived at the hotel ball-room, several hundred people were already circulating, talking in subdued tones. The overall mood was much more restrained than last night's mob scene at the Astrohall. She'd have expected a gathering of athletes to be a bit more lively.

"This reminds me of a Towering Texans meeting a friend once dragged me to. Except I'll bet not a one of these folks asks, 'Just how tall *are* you?' "

"I've gotten used to it."

"I guess I have too." Grammy had taught her to square her shoulders and be proud of her height. Conversely, she'd spent far too much time assuring men that she positively did not mind if they were shorter than she. Standing close to Gray, Garnet realized that she had minded after all.

"You're in the right place tonight."

Something clicked inside her, and she smiled up at him. "Yes, I surely am." It was probably a throwback to the Paleolithic era, but she felt very feminine, very secure with him beside her. And they did fit together divinely on the dance floor.

"Who's this you have in tow, Kincaid?"

She recognized Bennett Townsend, but waited for Gray to do the formalities. "Brindisi!" the florid-faced man bellowed. "For your sake, I hope you're not related to that worthless Lucky."

There was a moment of shocked silence. Garnet sensed Gray was about to do something rash that would only compound his boss's rudeness. "Worthless or not, Lucky's my father." And she would defend him if necessary.

Townsend poked his finger in her direction. "You

tell that sorry excuse for a man that if he ever shows his face in this town again, that's the day his luck runs out. I got a score to settle with that no-account gambler. Tell him."

He stalked off, leaving his mute little mouse of a wife to scurry along behind.

"I'm sorry." Gray's face was like a frozen mask. She wouldn't have wanted to be the object of his wrath at that moment. He looked capable of inflicting major damage.

"It isn't your fault he's a horse's rear. Everybody in town knows his reputation for being a loudmouth and a bully. Always threatening to move the team to another city or sell it to foreigners. I'm sure he makes your life miserable."

He gave her an odd, probing look, but didn't comment. "He must have your father confused with someone else, calling him a gambler."

"No, that's one thing he got right on the money."

"I see," he said, though he obviously didn't. Kincaids probably didn't mingle with professional gamblers.

"Well, at least we don't have to worry about a shoot-out on Westheimer," she said blithely. "Lucky hasn't set foot in Houston for years."

Gray did not seem relieved, but she was when he gestured at the head table, where a dozen people were taking their seats. "I think that's the cue to find our places."

They found a spot at a table with four other couples. Gray knew all of the men and three of their wives. As he performed introductions, Garnet was again struck by his flawless manners. He had an innate court-

liness rare in modern men. The outdated term "southern gentleman" kept flitting through her mind.

They endured a few brief speeches, nodding, laughing, and applauding at the appropriate times. Since
she couldn't wait to start talking to their tablemates,
Garnet fidgeted.

At last salads were served, and she said to the
woman on her left, "What a fantastic dress. I adore
that yummy shade of yellow, but it looks absolutely
virulent on me. Jaundice city."

"With your face and hair, I imagine you can get by
with wearing anything you like."

"You two forming a mutual admiration society?"
her seven-footer of a husband joked.

"Don't pay any attention to Stretch. He gets antsy if
the conversation centers on anything besides basketball."

Another woman, whom Garnet had immediately
diagnosed as shy, said, "Garnet's so unusual. Is it
your real name?"

"Mercy me, yes. Who could make up something
that outlandish?" She wiggled the fingers of her left
hand; the ring flashed green sparks. "A few hours
before I was born, my daddy won this big old bauble
in a poker game. He had no idea if it was real or not,
but his opponent was flat busted, so it was either
this stone or nothing."

She saw Gray's eyes narrow, but pressed on with
her story. "The guy said it was a tsavorite, a rare
and valuable kind of garnet. Being the superstitious
type, my father interpreted that as a sign I should be
named in honor of his winning."

"I'd think your mother would have objected to

naming you after a poker pot." Gray's disdain came through loud and clear.

"My mother is one of those poor, misguided women who believes her husband is always right." She tried to make that sound like an amusing eccentricity rather than a character flaw. "All she said was that it was a good thing he hadn't won a spinel or a zircon."

"Speaking of gemstones," one of the other women said, "I took in an interesting exhibit at the Contemporary Arts Museum this morning. Designs by Schlumberger, David Webb, and Verdure. Fabulous one-of-a-kind pieces."

"You're a newlywed," another wife commented with a laugh. "You get to indulge in the classy stuff. Wait until you're traveling with two little ones and it rains nonstop. Then you get to experience the wonder of animated dinosaurs."

"Oh, that is wonderful," Garnet piped in. "I took my kids and they loved it."

Gray's fork clanked against his plate. His eyes, which had warmed considerably over the past twenty-four hours, turned icy. Lost in their chilling depths, she barely heard someone across the table ask, "How old are they?"

"A couple have turned six. The rest are five."

When she saw eleven dumbfounded faces gaping at her, she laughed. "Maybe I need to start over. They're not mine personally. I was referring to my students. I'm a kindergarten teacher."

"A *kindergarten* teacher! But I thought—"

"That must keep you hopping," one of the fathers

guessed. "If yours are anywhere near as active as our five-year-old."

Garnet blessed the man for intervening at just the right time. Gray's outburst was so uncharacteristic that everyone must have noticed. "Oh, they're a handful, all right. But I wouldn't trade working with children for anything. Not even your high salaries," she added, pointing at each player in turn.

"Don't let her fake you out. What she really likes is playing dress up," Gray said, making an obvious effort to recover his composure. "Tell them about the cowboy routine."

Garnet never passed up an opportunity to plug the Rodeo, so she launched into a brief monologue about its history, the scholarship program, and the small but satisfying role she played in it.

"That's one of the reasons I'm here," she concluded. "Bennett Townsend and I are ganging up on Gray, trying to enlist him as a Rodeo volunteer. I plan to keep him in my clutches tonight until he's heard my best sales pitch."

The man on her right chuckled. "Better listen to what the lady says, Slowhand. Sounds like she means business."

Gray turned to her, lifting one side of his mouth in the quirky almost-grin that she was learning to like more each time it appeared. "Don't worry. I'm going to be very interested in everything the lady has to say tonight."

His words were heavy with promise, and so were his eyes. Garnet grabbed a program and fanned herself.

• • •

"Slowhand? I thought you were called Iceman." Garnet half turned in the seat as they sped away from the hotel. She was making a conscious effort to focus the conversation on Gray. She'd been in the spotlight all night, chattering a mile a minute, as usual.

Gray heaved a huge sigh. "Slowhand was a nickname some of my teammates hung on me. Luckily, the media never got hold of it. You can imagine the field day they'd have had with that one."

She could, and thinking about it constricted her chest and made her knees watery, even though she was sitting down. The small distance between them pulsed with suppressed energy. Her gaze locked on his hands, the way they dominated the steering wheel. "Why did they call you that?" she asked huskily.

"It meant I took time to set up, didn't rush my shots." He let the car roll to a stop at a red light. "I'm not real big on rehashing history. I'd much rather discuss why you didn't tell me what you do for a living."

Garnet bristled at the implied criticism. "I might have mentioned my job if you'd shown any interest in playing twenty questions." She didn't add that practically everything she had learned about him was courtesy of Stinky.

"Basketball is the only game I've ever been able to play. I have no talent for chatting up women."

She didn't believe that for a second. "I'm sure if you found a woman you deemed worth knowing, you'd come up with the appropriate small talk. I simply didn't qualify."

The car accelerated smoothly while he mulled that over. "There's a flaw in your theory. Why would I have gone out of my way to ask you to two things in one day if I see you as unworthy?"

Logical types were always the most difficult to argue with. "I don't think you consciously set out to ask me either time. It just slipped up on you, sort of like a virus." His prolonged silence told her she'd scored a hit. Being right in this case gave her little satisfaction.

"Do my original intentions really matter? Isn't the end result what counts?"

"Maybe. Depends on what you see as the end result."

In the hazy light of the Edloe Street overpass, she watched his facial muscles tense. "What I see is that we met each other roughly twenty-four hours ago. During that time I have danced with you—real close— been to your home twice, eaten a couple of meals with you, invited you to watch me in action, and seen you covered in mud."

Speechless, Garnet clutched the handgrip as Gray made a right turn on red at Bissonnet. His driving had gotten more aggressive with each word.

"You are the first woman I've asked to go *anywhere* since I landed in Houston, and furthermore, before the night is over, I'll no doubt ask you to go someplace else."

His admission was like a surprise gift and she cherished it. "Gray Kincaid, you were holding out. You know exactly how to chat up a woman."

He made another right, this one hard onto Auden, as if he'd done it a hundred times. "Don't delude yourself. I haven't the knack for flattery nor the desire to be charming. I'm not like the rest of your hangers-on."

"I would never mistake you for a hanger-on. But if you honestly think I'm swayed by flattery and charm, you're far less astute than I've given you credit for being."

The tires screeched as he swerved into the final turn for her street. "I'm not sure what to think anymore."

For a controlled man like Gray, that had to be the ultimate affirmation of vulnerability. "Sometimes, thinking too much causes trouble. Once in a while you just have to let go and see what happens. In other words, cut yourself some slack."

He wheeled into her driveway and killed the motor. "There's never been any room in my life for slack."

He pulled out the key and studied it. "Something tells me you and I don't punch the same holes in our precinct voting booth."

"Since when is that a prerequisite for anything?"

"Damned if I know."

"You swore."

"Did you think I didn't know how?"

"I wondered." She unclicked her belt, opened the door, and got out of the car. "Anything else you do that's against the rules?" She'd just upped the ante, like in a high-stakes poker game, and her pulse rate quickened as she waited for him to fold or call.

When he came around to her side, she could see a predatory light in his pale eyes. "Uh-huh. I teach smart-mouthed little flirts when to shut up."

The sensation of having backed herself into a corner heightened. Garnet shoved the door closed and hurried through the drizzle. " 'Little' is not a term to apply to me."

"A slip of the tongue."

He was standing so close, she could feel the warmth of him. It made her both wary and weak. She pawed in her purse for the keys. "I doubt if yours slips very often."

"No. My tongue usually does pretty much what I want it to."

She stifled a moan and crammed her key into the lock. The door sprang open. "Well, here we are. You've walked me to my door." Déjà vu, only this time she knew better than to taunt him as she had last night. "Thank you for a lovely evening."

"Garnet?"

She turned, her heart hammering at the sudden tension in his voice. It was all she could do to whisper "Yes?"

"This is where I kiss you good night."

Four

Before she could react, he had them both inside the hallway and the door shut. Before she could think, he pressed her against the wall, framed her face with his hands, and took her mouth with swift, passionate intent.

His kiss was not a gradual, gentle testing of the waters. It was a rampaging flood of sensations. Hot, wet, powerful. Total absorption, total possession, as if he had unleashed a potent force normally kept on a tight rein.

Her tame fantasies hadn't even come close to the unbridled reality of Gray's bold, insistent claiming. If this was an example of his tongue doing what he wanted, he was wickedly inventive. Curious, ravenous, it stroked and flicked and swirled, demanding her participation in the sensuous duel.

She surrendered her role as teacher and learned from him that kissing could elicit both sheer pleasure and exquisite torture. Pleasure so intense, it left her quivery. Torture, because she needed so much more.

His hands trailed down her neck, outward across her collarbones, around to her back, then dropped to her waist to bring her closer.

Instinctively, she draped her arms over his shoulders, molding herself to his taut, muscular contours. She swallowed his muffled sound of approval and granted him complete command of her mouth and of her senses.

Fitted together as securely as they were, she couldn't mistake the very masculine response of his body. The speed and intensity of it might have stunned her if her own reaction hadn't struck equally fast and strong.

For Garnet it was like nothing she'd ever experienced, overwhelming, irresistible, deliciously exciting. It made her daring. Pressing closer, she gave him a tiny, intimate nudge with her hips. The contact jolted her, like an electrical surge.

He groaned, jerked away, and plastered himself against the opposite wall. His eyes were closed, his chest pumped with the effort of breathing. "Lord, what's happening to me?"

Garnet lay one hand on the marble-top table to brace herself, and with the other touched her throbbing lips. "I assume that's a rhetorical question and you don't really need the textbook explanation."

His eyelids lifted, barely. "Why couldn't you be a little bit repressed and pretend not to notice?"

Garnet wasn't one for ultimatums, but she did believe in laying her cards on the table. "If that's what you want from me, Gray—pretense—there's the door."

Motionless, he regarded her while the banjo clock counted off endless seconds. At last he shook his head, and in a flash he was again so near, she could feel his breath on her face. "*This* is what I want from you."

She'd thought it impossible, but he made the second kiss deeper, wilder, more evocative. His fingers speared into her elaborate hairdo, sending pins flying and the long, thick strands cascading around them both.

Caution fled and time meant nothing. Gray became her center. He represented everything she had ever wanted or needed. He'd led her into a surreal world where he could hold her in thrall, fulfill every fantasy, satisfy her most secret desires.

And by doing so, he would dominate her, as her father did her mother. She could not give him that much power. "Gray, no," she murmured, dismayed at how little authority her voice held. "It's too much. Too fast."

He took a few seconds before releasing her. Shaken, she folded the satin cape tightly around her and sighed, "Well."

"Is that the best you can do? 'Well'?" His struggle for calm was visible and not entirely successful.

She clasped her shaky hands together and stared at them. "I started to say 'Wow,' then I figured that would sound immature and naive."

"Which, of course, you're not."

Her head snapped up; she searched his face for hidden meaning. To her the kisses had been transcendent. Maybe to a man like Gray they seemed ordinary, even boring. No, what she'd felt had definitely not been boredom. She might be inexperienced in certain areas, but that much she understood. "Being naive in this day and age is a dangerous risk. I'm aware of that as much as the next woman."

"I'm sure you are." The avid light in his eyes had

dimmed. He was under control and most likely searching for a way to downplay his temporary lapse. If he chose to apologize, she was going to have a fit.

True, she wasn't ready to finish what they'd started only moments ago. She needed to examine her feelings and intentions more objectively before making that decision. Gray was probably just as unsettled by the evening's unexpected conclusion. He'd need a break to regroup as badly as she did.

The clock bonged midnight, giving her the perfect opening. "Oops, you'd better take off before I turn into a werewolf or vampire or some other creepy critter."

He didn't respond to her weak attempt at humor, just opened the door and stepped out into the halo of her porch light. "You're right. It's past time."

It was difficult deciding how to answer such an obvious dismissal. Garnet's spirits plummeted.

He turned back around. "Other things keep interfering, and we still haven't had a chance to talk about the Rodeo. Want to try another game tomorrow? This time I'll be able to sit with you."

She released the breath she'd been holding. "I'd like that. A lot."

They agreed on a time, and after she locked the door behind him, Garnet switched off the lights and stood in the darkness, listening to him drive away. She couldn't recall ever being so apprehensive over whether a man would want to see her again or not. With Gray Kincaid she was venturing into uncharted territory in every respect.

She had spent a good portion of the last twenty-four hours with him. For much of the remaining time, he'd been on her mind. During that period he'd caused her to rearrange her schedule, reassess her priorities, and rethink her future.

She doubted Gray had made any such sweeping adjustments in his life. Still, he kept reverting to the Rodeo ploy as an excuse for asking her out, as if he needed justification. She interpreted that as a good sign. If he were merely interested in getting information, he could do it with a phone call.

For now, his motivation didn't matter. They would be spending Sunday together, which was enough to send her off to bed with happy thoughts filling her head.

By the following night she had even greater cause for optimism. Attending the game with Gray had been great fun, and he hadn't gotten unduly upset when she yelled at the officials, though she knew he'd have preferred a bit more restraint on her part.

Restraint wasn't her long suit, and if he couldn't find a way to accept the person she was, he wasn't the man for her after all. But deep down she felt confident, as she did in those poker games when she ended up winning big.

This time he left her at the door, eliminating any chance for a replay of last night's tempestuous scene. Garnet didn't mind. He wanted to, and there was no way his eyes could disguise the truth. That provided sustenance for her fantasies until she saw him again on Friday.

"My stars!" Garnet exclaimed, opening her front door. "You do own some clothes other than ties and dark suits. Good thing I didn't lay odds on it. Sure as shootin', I'd have lost my shirt."

Gray studied the fringed yoke of her red western blouse, then gave her a sexy half smile. "Too bad I missed my chance. That's one bet I'd be tempted to make."

Garnet silently blessed her Brindisi ancestors. Had she been born with typical redhead's skin, she'd be blushing to match her blouse. "Once in a while you surprise me, Mr. Kincaid."

"Lately I've started surprising myself."

Another good sign. She motioned him inside, performing a quick inspection of his jeans from the rear. They looked about a decade younger than hers, but they did right by his long legs and . . . the rest of him. "Are you ready to get your feet wet in Rodeo festivities?"

"Literally," he said, pointing to a pair of black boots, so shiny they had to be brand new. "Bennett's been hard on my case, insisting that I get involved in some aspect of the Rodeo. He's the boss, so here I am."

"And you, being a team player, always follow your boss's advice?"

She had meant the question to be teasing, but his expression turned grave. "There are instances when that's the only option. Anyone dealing with Bennett Townsend had better realize he's determined to have the final word."

Garnet caught the underlying edge in Gray's voice. It hinted at something serious brewing between the two men. But she was not in a position to pry or interfere. Yet.

She toed his gleaming boot with her old flat-heeled

red leather one. "You're going to mess those up royally. After months of monsoon, the ground is bound to be soupy."

He reached out to trace her silver metal collar tips. Instant warmth penetrated the thin cotton. "The boots will survive."

Garnet wasn't sure she would. Even his lightest touch sent her pulse rate soaring. She fumbled to buckle her navy suede waist pack, tossed a canvas jacket with painted barbed-wire design over one shoulder, and picked up a canvas tote bag. "Why don't we drive my urban assault vehicle? Save mucking up that fancy car of yours."

"It'll survive too. I'm going to have to work my way up to riding in your land yacht."

"Sugar lump, make fun of my old Caddy all you want. But anybody plows into Garnet is going to *comprehend* what it feels like to have an accident."

"I'll keep that in mind every time I get close to a garnet-green Eldorado," he retorted smoothly, skimming her ring finger with his thumb. "Come on, let's get this adventure on the road."

Knowing rush hour traffic on the freeways would be gridlocked, she directed him to Memorial Park via surface streets. But when they reached Memorial Drive, their progress halted. "It's the wannabe cowboys like us causing this bottleneck. All the trail riders reached the park by early afternoon."

"This morning I had to go out the Northwest Freeway for a meeting, and there on the frontage road was this long string of horses and wagons. I did a double take. Couldn't believe it."

"Only a newcomer would find that peculiar. It's just

part of Rodeo. With fourteen rides converging from all directions, they have to use highways to get here."

Gray inched the car forward. "It struck me as strange that this could be happening during the middle of a business day in the fourth-largest city in the country."

"This is Houston, remember? We take pride in doing things a little bit differently. To us this is the hot tamale, the big enchilada, the taco grande. You'll learn to look forward to all the hoopla if you stay a few years."

"I hope to stay more than a few years."

She hoped so too. "Then I guess you'll have to work very hard to make sure, since you think that's more important than luck."

"Believe me, I'm working harder than I ever have in my life." He fixed her with another of his solemn gazes, but this time it changed and became speculative. "On second thought, maybe it wouldn't hurt to try touching you. See if some of your luck rubs off."

Coming from any other man, Garnet would have passed off the remark as casual flirtation. There was nothing casual or flirtatious about Gray Kincaid, and when he came out with the unexpected it flustered her. It also made her consider challenging him to touch her all he wanted. Instead, she pointed to a side street. "Turn here. I have us a parking place reserved half a block up."

They still had to hike nearly a mile from her friend's driveway to the southside picnic grounds. Underfoot was as squishy as a bog and they passed quite a few trucks and trailers mired in muddy ruts. But as they approached the campsite, the laughter and conversation fragments they heard confirmed that no amount of water could dampen the trail riders' enthusiasm. After surviving days, or weeks, on the road, the saddle-weary travelers were primed to rest up and party down.

Smoke from campfires, grills, and cooking pots lay heavy on the damp air. Roasting meat sizzled, the aroma blending with spicy simmering chili, boiling coffee, and baking biscuits. One whiff and it was easy to see why the biggest crowds were clustered around the chuck wagons.

Gray stopped short when he first grasped the magnitude of the scene. "Good Lord! I had no idea there would be so many of them."

"Close to six thousand." Casting about for a familiar face, Garnet finally spied a fellow volunteer on horseback. Because he'd spent most of the day escorting the various rides to their spots, he was able to direct them to the approximate location of her brother's wagon circle.

Wading into the pack, she explained to Gray, "Ty's with the Salt Grass. They're the oldest ride, as well as the largest. They're also famous for serving up some of the best semiauthentic cowboy chow you've ever tasted."

"I don't know enough about cowboy chow to tell if it's authentic or not. You'll have to educate me."

"It'll be my pleasure." When the double meaning sank in, her breath caught and she looked up to see if Gray had noticed. Yes. How could she ever have believed his eyes were unreadable?

She blinked and shook her head. It was absurd to

fancy herself able to read Gray's thoughts as easily as if they were her own. She'd better take care, or her imagination was going to overtake reality and land her in big trouble.

Striving for normalcy, she waved at a couple stepping out of a deluxe travel trailer. "Catch up with you later," she called when they spotted her and waved back.

"Since when did cowboys trade in horses for luxury cars and motor homes?"

"No cowboy worth the name would ever get rid of his horse. It's just that now animals and machines have to coexist. Ranching, twentieth-century style."

"Ranchers, huh? Garnet, I've been studying these people as we walked by. A healthy percentage of them look like dentists or CPAs or trial lawyers dressed to pass as early Clint Eastwood."

"Good guess. We call 'em the mink and manure set. A lot of them grew up on the backside of nowhere and couldn't wait to escape to the city where they could make some real money. Once they do, the weirdest thing happens. They can't wait to rush back and buy their own little piece of nowhere. Then they spend most weekends driving there to do the kind of dirty work they went off to college to avoid."

"I can see someone maybe wanting to do that. But what's the point of taking part in this spectacle?"

Her boot skidded on the slick ground. Gray steadied her so quickly, she barely noticed. "You have to understand how deeply Texans revere land. They love riding on it, sleeping on it, eating on it. Settlers came here in the first place to claim it. I reckon devotion to land is the bedrock of just about every Texan's psyche."

"How about you? Do you have your own little piece of nowhere?"

"No, my brother was born with enough back-to-the-land urges for both of us. Grammy's house and yard are all I need." And she continued to need the security of them as badly as she had at the time her grandmother stepped in to provide the first permanence in six-year-old Garnet's life.

It always astounded her that lingering memories could still bring on shivers. Ever the gentleman, Gray draped his arm around her shoulders. "Cold?"

"I shouldn't be," she hedged. "Today was the first full day of sun in weeks. The air hasn't cooled yet."

"You promised it would clear off before the parade tomorrow morning. Does your luck extend to weather forecasting too?"

"Nope. That prediction was based strictly on past history. It never rains on the Rodeo parade."

They sloshed along the edges of several newly formed lagoons and came to a large clearing ringed by a stand of tall pines. "Oh, look. They're roasting a javelina." She tapped the shoulder of the man who was hand cranking a spit that held the meat suspended above a bed of glowing coals. "Smells yummy, Hector. Save me a bite, hear?"

"Will do." Hector touched the brim of his hat with one finger and kept on turning. "If you'll save me a dance."

"Spanish Trail Riders," she told Gray as they detoured around a wagon with bright yellow canvas and pots and pans hanging beneath it. "Most everyone will show up here at some point during the night. They put on the best dance in the park. Great music."

"How come you know so many people and so much about what goes on here?"

"Sweetie pie, my granddad rode the Salt Grass for years. When I was seven, he let me skip school and make the last day's ride with him. Since my initiation I've missed coming only a few years. Now it's one of the few chances I get to see my brother."

"He stays on his ranch most of the time?"

"Right. Dragging Ty off that spread is harder than wrestling steers. He hates coming to Houston, and I don't care to drive that far for a weekend."

"What about—"

"Oh, there he is now. Hurry!"

Gray watched her dash ahead and throw her arms around a tall man wearing a misshapen tan hat and a duster the color of oatmeal. Garnet's brother endured her eager hugs and kisses stoically while Gray disgusted himself by envying the man. He wasn't equipped to deal with conflicting emotions.

After last weekend he had decided to do the sensible thing and back off. But even a major disagreement with Bennett over the team's direction hadn't displaced Garnet in his mind. All week long he'd spent time he could ill afford visualizing things he had no intention of doing.

To make matters worse, he hadn't been able to stop himself from calling her every night. He'd tried to be relieved when she didn't answer on Monday. Tuesday irritation set in, and by Wednesday he was furious that she'd been out three nights running. None of it had discouraged him from picking up the phone on Thursday.

He wondered if she'd swallowed the line about his hanging around at Bennett's urging. Or what she would say if she knew that Bennett had ordered Gray to stay away from her.

Logic dictated that he should listen to Bennett. They both knew Garnet was the wrong kind of woman for him. But denying the attraction hadn't worked. Bottom line, being with her made him feel good. No danger in that.

People were always telling him he took life too seriously. Maybe it was time to heed their advice and ease up a little. So what if Garnet wasn't his type? In the past he sure hadn't set any records with women who were. Why not try something different? As long as he kept the thing in perspective, he could control it. No sweat.

Confident that he now had a fix on the situation, he ambled over to join the reunion. As Garnet performed introductions, her brother looked Gray straight in the eye. Not many men were tall enough to do that. All he said was, " 'Lo," but he did extend his hand.

Gray dipped his head and kept his greeting equally laconic. "Ty."

Garnet didn't act as though her brother's terseness was anything unusual. She babbled on and on about who said to tell him this, and what someone had done about that. Ty appeared to be listening, but without comment. Apart from their height, Gray could see no other similarities, in appearance or personality.

Tyler Brindisi was a man of economical movement and few words, Garnet a continual eruption of sound and motion. Her brother was no more like her than Gray was. *Opposites attract.* He'd never bought that theory. Until now.

"You persist in wearing this disreputable hat," she scolded. Grabbing it off his head, she made clucking noises and swiped at the stained felt. "Where's the new one I gave you for Christmas? Grammy'd say you look like something out of *The Grapes of Wrath*, but that's being too complimentary."

Ty just stood and waited for her to cram his hat back on, sending Gray a silent, long-suffering appeal.

"Have you talked to Mom and Lucky?" she asked, straightening his duster. She actually paused long enough to allow him to answer.

"They call at least once a week."

"Yes, but do you talk to them?"

"Sometimes."

"I assume they're after us for the same reason. What do you suppose is so all-fired important that they want both of us in Tahoe in March?"

"Beats me," Ty said with a shrug. "Doesn't matter. I ain't going."

Frowning, Garnet strummed her bottom lip with her index fingernail. "I decided the same thing at first, but now I don't know, Ty. They seem so earnest. Even Lucky makes it sound like they really want and need us to be there."

"So? When did they ever bother to come running when we needed *them*?"

Gray shifted, uncomfortable with what he'd overheard. Garnet's abstraction and Ty's animosity smacked of family conflict, something Kincaids went out of their way to avoid. He sure didn't want to be dragged into someone else's.

As if she read his thoughts, Garnet whirled to face him. "Excuse us, Gray. I didn't bring you here to hang out our dirty laundry. Anyway, now isn't the time. I guaranteed you some fun and maybe a learning experience or two. I'm going to shut up and deliver."

Her eyes rolled and her palm slapped her forehead. "I did it again. What's wrong with my mouth tonight?"

He gave the question his full attention, focusing on her lips, remembering how they tasted. "From where I stand, nothing at all."

"Ty-y," she said in a voice that sounded as taut as Gray's body felt, "why don't you take Gray to meet Cutter? He's under the impression that everyone's put their horses out to pasture."

Gray raised one brow to let her know the distraction didn't fool him. She had such a sassy, saucy tongue that it was bound to trip her up now and then. He liked watching her struggle to recover.

"You ride?" Ty asked skeptically.

"As a matter of fact, I do." Surprise registered on both Brindisi faces, but he didn't elaborate. Texans would probably distrust the skills of someone who'd learned them in hunt country.

"Oh, that's right. You're from Virginia. I'll bet you rode to the hounds while wearing hacking jackets, jodhpurs, and those snazzy little helmets."

"Hardly." While several relatives dressed exactly as she'd described, Gray had drawn the line at becoming quite that stuffy and traditional. By opting for a career in basketball, he'd rebelled further against a family heritage rife with judges and constitutional scholars. "I wouldn't like to try staying on a bareback bronc one-handed for eight seconds, but I can hold my own in the saddle."

Garnet's eyes lighted up. "You've been reading the Rodeo program I gave you. I was only kidding when I told you there would be a pop quiz."

"Yeah, but I don't want to risk getting in hot water with my teacher." Teasing, bantering, was foreign to Gray, yet here he stood taking on an expert. Some mysterious force must have possessed him. No, what had possessed him was a fascinating redhead with bewitching brown eyes and a tantalizing mouth. Resisting her charms required more willpower than he had.

"You want to wake up ol' Cutter and visit with him," Ty said, interrupting the byplay, "be my guest. Me, I'm heading for the grub."

"That sounds good to me," Gray agreed. "Garnet swears by your food, says it's the best on the trail."

"Men! Your stomachs always take precedence over everything else." She lifted the tote bag she'd dropped in order to get at Ty with both hands. "Let's find Shake, then. I can't wait to see what he's got cooking this year."

She charged into the crowd, leaving the two men to follow. "Ever feel like you're just drifting along in her wake?" Gray asked Ty in an undertone.

"Yep. Woman's got a lot of energy. Run a man ragged 'less he's good with a bridle."

Gray weighed the advice. "Soft hands, you mean."

Garnet's brother looked momentarily startled before a slow grin spread. "Maybe you do know a thing or two about horses, Kincaid."

"I understand you never rein them in hard enough to break their spirit."

"Good way to start. Instinct usually takes care of the rest."

Gray adapted easily to Ty's subtle, succinct form of communication. He got along best with people who chose their words carefully and used them sparingly. "My hands are good. So are my instincts." And he was probably overly optimistic to think an aptitude for basketball gave him any advantage in handling a woman like Garnet.

He watched her approach a chuck wagon and hug the stubby, bearded man bent over a cast iron cooking pot.

"Shake! You old miscreant, I'm hungry enough to consume the right side of a menu in one sitting. Whatcha got stirred up for us tonight? Rattlesnake stew?"

"Hidy, Miss B. For starters, I fixed a mess of beef tongue chili. Homemade tortillas too."

Gray came up beside her and she elbowed him in the ribs. "Ymm. Bet you can't wait to dig into that, huh?" She was an incurable tease, and beef tongue was too good an opportunity to pass up.

"Can't wait," he agreed.

"Hope you added tons of extra peppers. Gray has a taste for the spicy."

"That's right, Shake. Hot and spicy, just the way I like my women."

Garnet's mouth flew open. He could almost see

storm clouds forming in her eyes. Gray slipped an arm around her waist and gave her a hard squeeze. Then he spoke quietly in her ear. "You were asking for that. Admit it."

Lips pursed, she tilted her head to glare up at him. But she couldn't sustain her indignation for a fit of giggles. "Oh, all right, I admit it. I was doing my overbearing Texan funning a tenderfoot."

"What you have to learn about teasing is that it sometimes lands right back in your face."

She batted her lashes and smiled coquettishly. "Why, Gray, you're the one who said you never kidded, that you didn't know how."

"True. What you didn't take into account is that I'm a fast learner."

"Silly me. I guess you would be, a Rhodes scholar and all."

His arm dropped away from her waist. "Where did you hear that?"

"Stinky, of course. If I hadn't pumped him, I'd know next to nothing. Personal information coming from you is scarce as hen's teeth." She looked puzzled. "Is that Rhodes scholar business a secret or something?"

"No, I guess not." Gray had never analyzed why privacy was so important to him. Maybe it was just another family tradition, to guard the small details of life as closely as you did feelings.

"Snugglebunny, you can bet if Garnet Brindisi had been named a Rhodes scholar, we're talking full-page ad in both papers and TV coverage. I," she informed him with a naughty grin, "am a great believer in flaunting it if you got it."

"I," he replied sardonically, "would never have guessed. Too bad you have so little to flaunt."

She threw back her head and let out a deep, lusty laugh. "Holy cow. It really is time to feed you."

Gray had come here determined to prove himself a good sport, no matter what he had to endure. If that included sampling some exotic brand of chili, he'd bite the bullet. It ended up tasting pretty much like chili ought to. The grilled quail, Mexican rice, and charro beans were even better. With a flourish, Garnet brought out her home-canned dewberry and muscadine preserves to top Shake's biscuits, and like everybody else, Gray stuffed himself.

When he couldn't hold another bite, he settled back in a comfortable lawn chair, all set to listen to some guitar music. But Garnet wasn't having any of that.

"Come on," she coaxed, pulling him up despite his protests. "If we don't get a move on, you'll miss seeing everything on the tour."

She kept hold of his hand the whole time it took them to walk to the adjoining wagon circle. Entertainment there was a game of dominoes, the onlookers loud and bawdy in their assessment of the players. Several glanced up, recognized Garnet, and invited her to join in.

"Hey, everyone," she said, raising their joined hands. "Say hi to Gray Kincaid. I'm showing him the ropes. This is his first trail ride."

The whole group began to stir at once. The chorus of greetings was long and hearty.

Before he could react, four wiry men separated from the crowd and surrounded him. Before he could think, they hoisted him off his feet, each of them swinging him by either an arm or a leg.

"What the hell—" He was big and strong, but he couldn't best four-against-one odds.

On the count of three, they gave a mighty heave. Still cursing, Gray sailed through the air and landed on his back in a horse tank filled to the brim with frigid water.

Five

Garnet hopped backward to dodge the wave touched off by Gray's impact. "Uh-oh. I said the wrong thing to the wrong people." He strained to get up while the bystanders whistled, clapped, and shouted their approval.

When he uncoiled and stood, the water only reached his knees. He could easily step out of the tank. Someone pressed a towel into his hand. He made a fist around it, but didn't use it to dry himself.

His eyes, frosty as January in Juneau, hunted her. When he spotted his quarry, he came stalking. Looming over her, he tossed his head from side to side, spraying her with droplets, daring her to complain.

When she didn't, he said, "You set me up, sweet cheeks. It's going to cost you."

Even though he'd spiked it with sarcasm, that he would come back at her with one of her own style of endearments astonished Garnet. "I don't suppose I could persuade you to view this as a baptism of sorts."

"I'm almost sure you can't. But it'll be interesting hearing you try."

She seized the towel to dab at his face and neck. "Remember me telling you about my initiation when

I was seven?" He nodded once. "You've just participated in the traditional ritual. First-timers are rewarded with a dunking. It's official. You're a member of the club."

"*Rewarded* with a dunking? That's a privilege?"

"Indeed." She beamed up at him. Now that she knew he was more annoyed than angry, she could enjoy razzing him a little. "What's more, you didn't have to suffer days on horseback to earn the honor. That makes you about the luckiest guy in this park."

"What that makes me is drenched and cold, and you had better come up with some way to fix it real quick."

Spreading the towel across his shoulders, she again claimed his hand. "Your luck is holding, big boy. My brother could be your double in size and build. Let's go rustle up some of his extra clothes."

He didn't look thrilled, but hers was the only sensible alternative and he allowed her to tow him back toward Ty's camp. "You could have warned me," he said gruffly.

"If it had been planned as a prank, warning you would have spoiled the surprise. As it was, I coincidentally said the magic words, 'first time,' which they took as their cue. Really, I'm innocent of premeditation."

"Innocent?" He rotated his palm and meshed their fingers. "You'll have to do some serious convincing before I buy that one."

Garnet decided she could become addicted to the way his hand enveloped hers. It felt so solid, steady, and reassuring, symbolic of a strong and substantial man. For the first time ever, she longed to set aside her reluctance and cling to him. And she wanted him to need her equally.

The truth descended on her like an apocalypse. Her mission crystalized. It was up to her to free Gray of his own doubts and, by doing so, earn his trust and admiration.

A tall order, but one she was committed to filling.

After locating Ty, Garnet pilfered his meager store of clean clothes and borrowed a nearby motor home so Gray could change. When he emerged from the small bedroom at the rear, she indulged herself in a leisurely appraisal. "Just between the two of us, you should stick to athletic shoes instead of boots. And I like faded jeans better."

"I've noticed." He gave her legs an up, down, and back up look that was so incredibly hot it ought to have carried a DANGER: COMBUSTIBLE warning.

He stood in the center of the small living area, so imposing that the already close confines of the compact vehicle shrank further. Inside her, a sudden, restless desire flared. She snagged a denim jacket from beside her on the couch, leaped up, and started edging her way to the door. "You'll need this." She held out the jacket.

He didn't budge. "Aren't you forgetting something?"

"Oh, yes. The wet clothes." Still flushed, she darted over to rummage around under the sink until she found a trash bag. "You can put them in this."

"I wasn't talking about my wet clothes."

"What, then?" She worried a hangnail. Picked at the zipper tag on her waist pack. Studied a comic strip anchored to the refrigerator with a magnet. Anything to avoid meeting Gray's gaze.

"Aren't you curious to find out what my initiation is going to cost you?"

"I assumed you made that threat, uh, in the heat of the moment."

He advanced on her; the cabinet at her back prevented retreat. "I never make threats, Garnet. Not in the heat of the moment, not anytime."

Talk about heat. She was inundated by it, barely able to get out "I'll remember that."

"Good. Now it's time for you to pay up." His index finger probed the seam of her lips. They parted. She couldn't have breathed otherwise. The feathery play of his finger moistened the tip, and when he licked it, the effect was so powerful she had to look away.

The initial brush of his mouth over hers was gentle; she could hardly feel it. His delicate repetition of the pattern sensitized her unbearably. She couldn't suppress a blissful moan. He increased the pressure slightly, but the contact remained light, undemanding. And because of that, she surrendered without hesitancy, leaning into him.

Only then did she feel the languid slide of his tongue against hers, an agonizingly sweet invasion. This kiss was the exact opposite of their first in every way, save one. For all its tenderness, it was every bit as devastating.

Gray pulled away a fraction and his eyes blazed with masculine hunger. "I want you, Garnet."

His admission, a hoarse blend of frustration and resignation, made her head buzz like a straight shot of hundred-eighty-proof alcohol.

"You know I do."

"Yes," she whispered, aware that his willingness to

verbalize the confession somehow strengthened the bond between them.

"I'm not the type to rush—" He cut himself off with a short laugh. "Hell, listen to me. I'm already rushing this something fierce. Better shut up before I make some rash promise I don't stand a snowball's chance of honoring."

"And you *are* a man who honors his promises, aren't you, Gray?" She was positive of that on a very basic level.

"Yes. Always."

His avowal touched off a chain of internal tremors. Here was a man from a different mold than the nineties type she and all of her friends professed to be seeking. The polish and poise concealed tougher stuff, an old-fashioned, uncompromising, to-the-bone integrity.

She needn't look any further. In Gray, she'd found the kind of man that subconsciously she had spent her entire life searching for. The discovery made today one of the luckiest days of her life.

"How do you feel about a wedding?"

"I beg your pardon?"

Garnet chuckled at his trapped-with-no-way-out look. "Two people from the Prairie View Trail Ride are getting married tonight. Shake told me about it at dinner. They'd like as many as possible to attend the ceremony. You game?"

"Uh, sure. Why not?" In two steps he reached the door and unlatched it. "I'm game."

Garnet and Gray were among the first outsiders to join the couple's circle of friends and fellow riders. Assembling on either side of a red carpet, they stood in two groups, much as they would have in a church. A pair of five-branch candelabra held lighted tapers, their flames undulating in the slight breeze. An accoustic guitarist played something celebratory.

More people converged. Those present began speaking in hushed tones. Then a robed minister and a pair of attendants took their places at the head of the group. As soon as the guitarist segued into the "Wedding March," the bride and groom proceeded down the makeshift aisle, hands already joined.

Unabashedly sentimental, Garnet became immersed in the beauty of the moment. This was by no means a traditional setting, but the simple purity of the music, the reverence of the witnesses, and the vows, as solemn and moving as any ever said in a chapel, were lovely to her.

A tear spilled from her right eye. She dashed it away with one finger, but another escaped, followed by still more, unleashing a torrent. Sniffling, she watched the exchange of rings, momentarily startled when Gray thrust a crisp, white handkerchief into her clenched fingers. With one hand, she used the linen to blot her face, clutching at his hand with the other.

She looked into his eyes and made a wish, hoping, praying that someday he would wish for the same thing.

The pastor pronounced the pair man and wife and sanctioned a kiss. That accomplished, champagne bottles materialized from all directions, the sound of popping corks supplying a different sort of music. Toasts echoed; the crowd turned giddy. And the bridal couple invited everyone to share in the joy of their wedding dance.

Additional musicians joined the guitarist. The band struck up "Waltz Across Texas." Gray gathered her close, and Garnet was again struck by how supremely right she felt in his arms. "Why are you looking at me funny?" He touched the corner of one eye and she swiped at her cheek. "I guess my mascara's drippy, I must resemble a clown."

"No. You look . . . fine. But I never would have cast you as the sentimental type who cries at weddings."

"Has it occurred to you that you don't know me very well at all?"

"Yes. I've thought about that quite a bit. But I don't see it as too big a problem. As I told you, I'm a fast learner."

"Where were you Friday night? I tried to get in touch with you at six o'clock and you were already gone."

Gray found Bennett Townsend's imperious tone almost as offensive as he did the noxious cigar smoke. He especially objected to being summoned for this grilling to Bennett's downtown office first thing Monday morning. "I had plans that night."

"I hope to God they didn't include that Brindisi woman." He spat out her name as though it tasted bad.

Gray fought down the urge to tell Bennett to go straight to hell. He knew that defending Garnet and the time he spent with her would only further aggravate an already unstable situation between him and his boss. He said nothing.

"Tried to reach you all day Saturday and Sunday too. Don't you ever stay at home?"

"I took your advice. Went to the Rodeo parade Saturday and to the opening performance yesterday."

"Oh." Momentarily appeased, Bennett blew out several puffs of toxic smoke. "What'd you think?"

"Interesting. It'll have to wait until the season's over, but I'm probably going to volunteer." His decision had not come as a result of Bennett's high-pressure tactics, though he was sure the man would interpret it that way.

"Well, good. Way things look with the team right now, I figure you won't be worrying about any postseason games."

Here we go again. Gray hoped he could stay cool. It wasn't going to be easy with Bennett attacking him on both personal and professional fronts. "There's still half a season left. I'm confident we can make it into the play-offs."

"Hmmph. You must believe in miracles. It won't happen any other way with this bunch."

Gray forced himself to breathe slowly and choose his words. "No, I don't believe in miracles. Championship teams aren't built overnight. You have to do it piece by piece, with smart draft choices and drilling in the fundamentals and discipline."

"I'm fed up with waiting. You need to take action."

Bennett assumed that some dramatic gesture would not only shake up the team and get the members playing better, it would placate the media and fans. So far Gray had been able to stall him. At each meeting, however, he became more insistent. "The won-lost percentage is better than at this time a year ago."

"The numbers still aren't good enough."

"But they are improving steadily."

"I want better. Dammit, I deserve better. You're the fair-haired boy. I hired you to do something!"

As if the eighty-hour weeks he'd been putting in since last summer didn't count. "I am doing something. We have more scouts looking at more draft prospects than ever before. The assistant coaches have instituted new practice routines. We're studying other teams for off-season trade prospects."

"They still lose the close games. My poor little Janey can't even watch them anymore. Says it just makes her too nervous and depressed."

Gray remembered Garnet's description of the Townsends and figured the cause of poor little Janey's nervousness and depression was being married for so many years to a horse's rear. "Dropping the close ones is mental. We're working on that problem too. They'll come together."

"But it's taking too long."

"Just be patient a little longer," he said with more confidence than was warranted.

As Bennett was about to let loose with another complaint, his secretary stuck her head in the door, reminding him that he had to leave for an appointment. Gray got up to go, feeling as though he'd been granted a reprieve. But Townsend halted him in his tracks with a parting shot. "You mind what I'm telling you about that woman. She's nothing but gambler's spawn. Stay away from her. She'll only cause you trouble, which you've got plenty of already. Start carrying on with her and I'll see that you have even more."

Gray seethed all the way to his car. He didn't take

kindly to threats in any form, and Bennett was notorious for issuing them. Before signing on as general manager, he had pointed out to Townsend that the Wildcatters were two, possibly three, years away from winning it all. There were no shortcuts around that fact.

Barreling out of the parking lot, he drove with a heavy size-thirteen foot all the way back to the Summit. The speed did nothing to ease his temper. He flopped down in his chair and angled it to stare out the window. Until he calmed down, work was out of the question.

He hated losing control, which happened increasingly often these days. Bennett, Garnet, each bedeviling him in their own way.

When his boss complained like a petulant child, Gray felt like shouting at him to grow up and butt out, to stick to oil, where he'd made the fortune that enabled him to dabble in basketball. He knew nothing about the inner workings of a team, yet he insisted on calling the shots. His constant harassment made Gray's job more difficult by the day.

Harsh reality dictated that Gray be accountable to the man. He had to keep juggling all the balls or else he would fail miserably at the goal he most desperately wanted to attain.

But what really infuriated him was the nerve of Bennett to meddle in his personal life. No one had ever presumed to tell him what to do or whom to see. Even his father, after instilling in Gray the rules of proper and acceptable conduct, had assumed he would always do the right thing.

Bennett's denunciation of Garnet, whom he'd just

met, bordered on fanaticism. Gray replayed their first meeting and his own opinions of her. Sure, she was flamboyant and she sometimes expressed herself too candidly. But right away he'd discovered that underneath the flash, she was a warm and caring person. She loved kids and animals. Made homemade jam and talked to flowers as she planted them. None of that justified Bennett's wrath.

Something about her father's gambling really set Townsend off. Gray agreed that the pastime seemed a bit suspect, a bit seedy. But he couldn't condemn Garnet for a vice that had nothing to do with her. From all indications, she rarely saw the man she called Lucky.

Gray felt like the worst kind of cad for not defending her against his boss. It would have been the right and honorable thing to do. But Bennett had him between a rock and a hard place, and he was feeling the pinch.

All day long the threats continued to gnaw at him, almost as much as the feeling that he'd betrayed Garnet with his silence. By the time he got ready to go home at seven, he didn't bother with rationalizations. He drove straight to her house. Although he didn't plan to reveal the whole sordid tale, he could do something to make up for his sin of omission.

In addition to easing his conscience, this visit meant he didn't have to wait until Friday to see her.

But she wasn't at home. Frustrated, he went to get something to eat, then returned. No sign of her or the old Cadillac. He left again, this time to get the car gassed up, washed, and waxed, a useless exercise when the forecast called for more rain. About nine-thirty he came back and found the house still dark.

Skulking around like a suspicious lover was juvenile. Disgusting. Deciding to hell with it, he took off for his condo. Once there, his agitation continued to build until all he could do was pace and fume. At eleven he finally said to hell with that too and dug out his keys.

Might as well face it. Like a besotted fool, he was going to stake out her house until she showed up. And then they were going to get a few things straight.

Driving home from a poker game at the Whitts, Garnet toted up figures on her mental calculator. Although tonight's winnings didn't rival the bonanza of several weeks ago, she could make a nice deposit to the scholarship fund.

If she only had more resources. So many girls needed encouragement and financial assistance. Each year Garnet's group had to turn down many deserving applicants and that broke her heart. She supposed it was naive, but she wanted to give everyone a chance. Maybe she ought to expand her circle of card-playing buddies, improve the odds. Or . . .

For the first time, she contemplated a trip to Vegas where she might hit it really big. That led to thoughts of Tahoe and her parents' repeated requests that she visit them. "Hmm, there are casinos in Tahoe. I could accomplish two things at once." But did she really want to do either?

Garnet hadn't set foot in a casino in close to twenty

years. The prospect of returning made her queasy. She did not look back on the gambling life with fond memories.

Of course, this time it would be different. She'd grown up and was now in control of her life. Not at the mercy of a man like Lucky. She could tolerate the apprehension if the reward meant helping that many more.

Engrossed in her plans, she narrowly missed clipping the rear bumper of a parked car that almost blocked her driveway entrance. "Fool," she grumbled before the sedan's overhead light came on and a familiar figure unfolded.

She jammed on the brakes and ran the power window down. "Gray! You're the last person I expected to be keeping a midnight vigil here."

"I imagine so." He sounded irritated.

"Don't tell me I stood you up. I would never have forgotten if we'd made plans."

"We didn't have a date."

Dating was such a trivial term for what was developing between them. "Then why—"

"That's what I want to know. Why is it midnight and you're just getting home?"

Not irritated. Angry. Gray playing the irate cross-examiner struck Garnet as so incongruous she almost laughed. His forbidding expression changed her mind in a hurry. "Let me get this straight. You're demanding I account for my whereabouts tonight?"

He flattened his palms on the car and stuck his face close to hers. "If you want to put it that way, yes."

"Can you come up with some other way to put it?"

He straightened and took a couple of backward steps. Arms crossed, he assumed a defensive stance. "I just want to know what you're up to."

"That is not a politically correct male attitude."

"Screw politically correct," he thundered, in her face again. "Tell me where you were. Who you were with."

Dumbfounded, Garnet recoiled. Gray never shouted, never so much as raised his voice. What was going on? "I spent the evening at Dewdaddy and Mrs. Whitt's house. A few others were there, too, all friends of my grandparents. I'm sure they'll sign a sworn statement if necessary."

This time when he backed away, he seemed unsteady. He was also breathing heavily. "You weren't with another man . . . doing . . ." Hands crammed in his pockets, he pivoted toward his car. She heard him mutter, "Damn," followed by a second, louder, "damn!"

"There is no one else, Gray. I can't imagine what gave you the idea there might be."

"*You* gave me the idea. The way you look and dress and move. You're so . . . spectacular, and men, well, they pick up on that. All men. When you're around, every other woman sort of fades from view. I don't know how to cope with the attention you draw."

She did laugh then, partly from relief, partly from elation. A jealous Gray was as staggering as a shouting one. Not that she wished to encourage either. "I'm flattered that you see me that way. But I think you've exaggerated my charms by a good bit."

"You think so, huh?" He swiveled around to scowl at her. "Then how come there's always a crowd of drooling males around you? How come you have a smile and something to say to every one of them? And why do you give the impression that their attention will be rewarded?"

Magnificent in his outrage, he appeared to grow even taller. Garnet knew it was time to draw the line, but she couldn't quite muster the proper degree of indignation. "Mrs. Youngblood is already peeking through her curtains. At this rate we'll wake the whole neighborhood. Why don't we finish our discussion inside?"

He blew out a huge sigh. "That's the worst suggestion I've heard today. And, trust me, since this morning, I've heard some beauts."

"You don't want to come in? Why? Afraid you might get your hands on me and—"

"I'd like to get my hands on you, all right." His eyes widened in horror, as if he couldn't believe what he'd just said. Then he covered his face, kneading it with spread fingers. "I don't like losing my temper, Garnet, and you've made me do it more than once."

If that's how he saw this minor blowup, his definition of losing his temper differed from hers. He hadn't exactly gone on a rampage. "Holding everything in all the time is unhealthy. You need to vent your hostilities periodically."

"I try to avoid hostility in the first place. Keeps life simpler. Tonight I went off the deep end. I'm not sure why. All I can do is apologize." It started to sprinkle. He made a great show of zipping his windbreaker and turning up the collar.

Garnet figured he was trying to work up to his departure with a minimum of fuss. That done, he would spend the next few hours condemning himself for resorting to the type of behavior most people wouldn't even question. She knew the pattern well.

Like her brother, Gray had trained himself to prevail over ordinary human weaknesses. On those few occasions when the system failed, they automatically went internal.

"I'll accept your apology, but only if you admit that it was okay to react in the first place."

"No, my behavior was excessive. Inappropriate."

Behavior? Had she returned to Psychology 101? "Shoot, if I'd been waiting all night in a car, courting a charley horse, and you finally turned up at midnight, I can guarantee I would have been ready to tear a strip off." She twirled a strand of her long hair around her pinky. "By the way, you look adorable when you're in a snit."

His mouth twisted in disdain. But within seconds it relaxed into his trademark almost-smile. "I can't believe you said that."

"Sure you can. I've said worse. Besides, it jarred you out of your funk, didn't it?"

"I guess. But now I'm just getting wet, another thing that happens too often around you."

She reached out and swirled her hand in a fingerpainting motion through the water beading the front of his jacket. The taut resistance of his stomach kindled a tingle in her own. "You could come in and let me dry you off, warm you up, tell you a bedtime story."

He groaned, and she thought it sounded very masculine, very seductive. "One of these nights your sassy mouth's going to get you in too deep."

"You told me you didn't make threats."

"I don't." Oh, she loved those rare sexy grins of his. "Which means you'd better take care to guard your . . . rear." And she loved the way his voice turned husky with promise. It made her insides go all warm and fluid.

"I'll take care, baby cakes."

"Start now." He thumped the top of her car, giving her a go-ahead signal. "See you Friday."

"I can't wait." She never liked saying good night to Gray, but she lifted her foot off the brake and the car coasted up the driveway.

Before she made it to the door, he was beside her again, his hand on her shoulder. "Just one last thing, Garnet. What *were* you doing tonight?"

"The same thing I've been doing a couple of times a month for the past four years. Playing poker." She waved her purse at him. "This was a slow night, but I still won almost four hundred dollars."

"You did *what?*"

Six

Gray's hand jerked from her shoulder so fast, it left Garnet swaying. "You spent the past five or six hours playing poker? For money?"

"I've never seen much point to the game unless there's a payoff."

He looked panic-stricken. "But that's gambling."

"Well, yes, I suppose it is, technically. Dewdaddy prefers to think of it as a small game of chance among friends. That's all it is, really."

Now he looked confused, or maybe ill. Shoulders slumped, he gazed off in the distance. He said something under his breath. She couldn't hear the words and thought it was probably a good thing. When he spoke, he kept his eyes averted. "The envelope Mr. Whitt gave you at the dance, was that . . ."

"My jackpot," she said when he appeared unable to settle on the proper term. "He hadn't brought that much cash the night we played."

"Then you're a gambler. Just like your father."

He made it sound like a punishable offense. "Apart from inheriting his lucky streak, I am not at all like my father."

"If you—"

"Be quiet and listen. You're the one tossing out accusations and comparisons. Lucky is a high roller, not some sleazy, down-and-out bum living hand to mouth. For over thirty years he's traveled the globe, playing at the poshest casinos and parlaying his luck and skill into a damned good living."

"But no—"

"I said listen. When Ty and I were little, we stayed in suites at the finest hotels, ate at big-name restaurants, hung out with the beautiful people, and saw sights all over the world." She omitted that they had both been miserable.

"My father believes in going first-class—he can afford to—and I'll bet he's worn out more tuxedos than all your fancy Virginia friends combined."

"None of that changes the fact that he's a gambler. Dress it up any way you want, it's still hard to defend as a respectable lifestyle or a responsible way to raise children."

He was only asserting what Garnet had told herself countless times. But coming from Gray, it made her angry and it hurt. She touched her temple, could feel the pressure hammering at her from inside. "What gives you the right to pass judgment on my family or anything I do?"

"It isn't that I'm passing judgment exactly. But Garnet, gambling . . . surely you can see it's a dangerous addiction. It can ruin your life."

"Let's get one thing straight. I am not addicted. If you want to know the truth, I don't even like it very much. I just happen to have a talent for it."

"You're saying you can take it or leave it?" A spark of encouragement brightened his eyes before it died. "Then why do you take part on a regular basis in something you have no real interest in?"

"Because teacher salaries are disgracefully low and

I have no inherited wealth. In short, I need the money."

"Debts, is that it? You've had some unforeseen expenses, and gambling is your only source for getting the money fast?" His hands wrapped around her upper arms. "I'll give it to you. A loan. Just tell me how much you need and you'll have it by morning."

"Gray, you don't understand. This is something I want to do myself. No, I *have* to do it on my own."

His grip tightened and he gave her a little shake. "Is someone threatening you? Did you borrow from the wrong people? For God's sake, Garnet, let me help."

"Shh, you're overreacting again. I can't imagine what's possessed you tonight. Calm down and I'll explain." In a hushed voice she told him about the scholarship program her businesswomen's chapter supported and why she was so committed to its growth.

He didn't respond for a long time, just kept shaking his head. "How can I argue that what you're doing isn't admirable and generous? But I also can't help thinking there must be a better, more acceptable way than gambling to finance it. We're not talking millions."

"I'm sure the amount I need is trifling to you and all the deep-pockets folks you associate with." Though she sounded testy, she felt like crying. She and Gray inhabited contrasting worlds. The differences, particularly in their financial status, had not intruded before. Now it was clear that money represented a huge chasm dividing them.

"We obviously don't see eye to eye on this issue, so it seems pointless to continue the discussion. Besides, it's late and I have to get up early. I'm going in."

"Garnet, wait."

"No, Gray. I don't want to talk about it anymore." She walked purposefully to the door, relieved that he didn't try to stop her. Once inside, she collapsed onto the hall bench, too tired to go any farther. Her grandmother used to complain about old bones. Garnet wondered if Maggie had felt the way she did right now, old and weighted down.

Gray's strong negative reaction to her poker playing had taken the wind out of her sails. She simply couldn't understand his objection, especially after she'd clarified where she played and with whom. It wasn't as if she lived a fast life or frequented disreputable places or mingled with unsavory characters.

No, his disapproval went deeper than that, and it was based on some factor not subject to reason. Reticent as Gray was, she might never find out, much less be able to refute it.

Garnet rose and shuffled into the bedroom. Her brain was too jumbled to grapple with the problem tonight. First thing in the morning she'd tackle it and formulate some plan for winning him over to her side.

She didn't get a chance to think about it at all. The ringing phone woke her first. It didn't shock her to hear Gray's voice, because only seconds before she'd been dreaming that he'd called.

"I wanted to make sure you're all right."

"I am terrific," she said, disgustingly cheerful because he cared enough to check. For a few seconds right before she fell asleep, Garnet had fretted that he might just wash his hands of her and her—how would he term it?—problem? "I was in the midst of a wonderful dream. About you. And me of course."

He cleared his throat. "It bothered me to leave you like that last night, with nothing settled."

"Something tells me we could have stood out there till dawn and not settled anything. It also tells me this is an area where we're going to have to agree to disagree and let it go at that." She hesitated before adding, "If we're to continue seeing each other."

"Would you rather not?"

She could guess that his eyes had gone quite cold, to match the soft, wintry tone of his voice. "Get serious. I'm a lot harder to ditch than that, Gray Kincaid, and you'd better not forget it."

Garnet told herself that wasn't a sigh of relief she heard. "I'm struggling to get a handle on whatever is happening between us, but I seem to be making a hash of it."

"Get a handle? Can't you just relax? Wait and see what develops?"

"No, that's not my way. I need to know what's in store for me, for us, exactly where we're headed."

She had never understood why men persisted in trying to analyze and complicate anything related to feelings. "Don't look to me for the answer, because I haven't a clue."

"Don't you care where this is leading us?"

"You bet I care." She knew what she *wanted*, but with an elusive man like Gray, one had to let the pot simmer before it could boil. "In our case I think nature has taken the driver's seat and we'll do better if we just enjoy the scenery along the way."

He took enough time to prepare a rebuttal. Instead, he said, "That is a very illogical, haphazard approach." Another meaningful pause. "But since logic hasn't worked for me so far, I might as well try it your way for a while."

"Stick with me, sweet pea. I'll teach you a thing or two yet."

"I've already learned a thing or two."

As she laughed at the ironic humor in his voice, her old-fashioned Big Ben alarm clock clanged its wake-up call. "Speaking of learning, time for me to look sharp. Shake's paying his yearly visit to my class today to demonstrate campfire cooking. I have to get there early and help him set up."

"Another round of his beef tongue chili, huh? Better not tell your students what they're eating. They might not be as gullible as I was." She heard papers shuffling. "Before I let you go, are we still on for Friday?"

"If you're still game." When he assured her that he was, she added, "Now Gray, please remember that I did give you advance warning."

Gray furtively cased the hall as he unlocked his front door. "Cool move," he mumbled, mocking his guilty conscience. Did he think someone was going to leap from behind a potted palm and arrest him for truancy?

He'd never played hooky. Not until Garnet had tempted him. Kincaids took their responsibilities seriously, whether it be school, job, or philanthropy. Today's outing might optimistically be classed as the latter. But he had a feeling Bennett would foam at the mouth if he ever found out the reason for Gray's absence. Every time he had to contend with Townsend, the man grew more rabid. About the team, but even more so on the subject of Garnet.

Unless he'd hired a spy, Bennett had no proof that Gray had even seen her since being ordered to stay away from her. But that detail didn't stop the tirades. Gray had become adept at shutting him out, and at ignoring his own reservations. Not even the bombshell about her gambling had diminished his need to be with her.

Need. Garnet had taught him a new definition of that word, taught him that he wasn't immune to strong emotions and powerful desires. At times he got so stirred up, all he could do was curse his loss of the inner calm that had enabled him to weather life's hassles so easily.

Then Garnet would laugh or tease him or drive him wild with one of her soul-deep kisses. The Iceman might never have existed.

Gray stripped off his suit and tie and dropped the white shirt in a bag for the cleaners. He dug out basketball shoes, a pair of jeans, and a blue-and-white-striped shirt. The city was caught up in "Go Texan" days, but that didn't mean he had to follow the crowd and dress like a cowboy. Going to the Rodeo several times was a big enough concession for his first year here.

Fifteen minutes later he parked in the lot of Garnet's school and walked around to the front of the building where a couple of buses waited. He braced one hand high on the yellow side and stared at traffic, lost in the past.

How many hours had he spent on buses during all those basketball seasons? Too many to count. That was one thing he didn't miss. That and the constant travel, the boredom of waiting around to play a game, and especially sleeping in a different bed almost every night.

"Hello, handsome," a sultry voice behind him said. "Take you for a ride in my kiddie car?"

He started, then glanced over his shoulder at Garnet. It always amazed him how she could manage to look sexy and impish at the same time. "You've been taking me for a ride since the moment we met."

"It's been interesting, too, admit it."

Interesting, and something else he couldn't define. "I admit it."

She winked, and he wanted to pin her against the bus and plant a long, wet kiss on those delectable lips. As if she'd read his mind, she winked again and murmured, "Hold the thought. We've a whole lovely weekend ahead of us."

Gray closed his eyes and sucked in a deep breath. He didn't know how much longer he could endure hours with her and not touch her as intimately as he wanted.

She was wearing boots, a denim riding skirt, and a white blouse with five kinds of cattle lined up the front over the buttons. The effect on him was as potent as black silk, skin, and expensive perfume.

After checking with the bus driver, Garnet left to get her class. She returned in minutes shepherding her brood of sixteen. They surrounded her, skipping alongside or tugging at her hands. Even from a distance Gray could tell that every one was bursting with energy and excitement.

It hit him that he knew next to nothing about handling children, had rarely been around them. Given that, only an idiot would volunteer for this duty.

Or a man on the brink of taking a very big leap.

Garnet came to stand beside him as she supervised the loading. "Remember to sit on the side behind the driver. Mrs. Zaleski's students will take the opposite side."

"I don't see how you can keep so many under control inside a classroom. It must be a nightmare trying to keep track of them in the midst of thousands of people and animals."

"That's why we have a one-to-four ratio of chaperones. This is my fifth year, if you count student teaching. No catastrophes so far." She bent and extended an arm in front of a little blond boy about to board. "Whoa there, Stuart, my sugar plum. Where's your name tag?"

The boy whipped off his Astros cap and showed her the inside. "So I don't lose it."

"Aren't you clever. But what if you misplace your cap, and I get careless and lose you?" With a minimum of fuss, she transferred the pin-on tag to his shirt pocket and patted him onto the bus. "Just be sure you don't give anyone the shirt off your back."

Gray marveled at how ingeniously she'd solved the problem without making Stuart think he had done anything wrong.

When her class was loaded, a second group of kindergartners and their chaperones filed out to fill the rest of the seats. Gray was the only male over six, and he felt a little like Gulliver. Ducking his head, he climbed the two steps.

After raising her hand for quiet, Garnet spoke in an

unusually soft voice, "Okay, all my honeybees, listen up. This is Mr. Kincaid. He's new to Houston and has never been to the Livestock Show, so I invited him to go with us. But he's helping me out, too, and if he asks any of you to do something, please pay attention as you would if I asked."

"Wow!" exclaimed a little girl several rows behind them. Her head dropped back in order to take in all of Gray. "Did you find a husband, Miss B?"

"Help me," he mumbled, sinking into one of the front seats Garnet had reserved for him. It was going to be a long afternoon. Staring at his shoes, he heard the amusement in her voice when she answered. "Where did you get that idea, Laurel?"

" 'Cause my dad said you're so tall you'd probably never find a husband, and I just wanted to tell him if you did."

"Well, lamb chop, you be sure to tell him I'm still looking."

Gray was torn between laughing and running for cover.

The ride to the Astrohall took about twenty minutes, during which Garnet did a magic trick, told a cowboy story, and played I Spy word games. Then she began to sing, "There is a state and it is great and Texas is its name-o." The kids chimed in to spell "T-E-X-A-S," each repetition louder. Before he knew it, Gray was singing along to the tune of "Bingo," as captivated by her spirit as everyone else.

She had once said she had no discipline problems because every child was interested in something. The secret lay in finding out what and using that as a teaching tool.

She'd also stated that learning ought to be exciting, and excited students were rarely quiet. If the decibel level inside the bus was any indication, some heavy learning was taking place.

Funny . . . he couldn't recall ever having a teacher who looked, or acted, like Miss B.

When they arrived at the Astrohall, they checked in and were assigned FFA guides. "That stands for Future Farmers of America," Garnet told her class, "and they're students just like you. But they live on farms and will be able to tell us all about the animals."

The teenage girl began by talking about how each animal has its own personality, just like people, and that animals can be friends, just like people.

"This is another program the Rodeo promotes," Garnet whispered to him. "It seems incredible, but many of these children have never seen farm animals, except in books or movies. So country kids take city kids by the hand and educate them."

"Is there anything that goes on in the Rodeo you don't know about?"

"Not much. I grew up surrounded by it. My grandparents spent years volunteering and eventually worked their way up to chairing committees. I guess it's only natural that I'd follow in their footsteps."

He thought back to the dance and how he'd immediately dismissed her as a shallow, flirtatious party girl, an assumption he'd since abandoned. "You really are committed to this, aren't you?"

"To all forms of education, you mean? Yes, I've pretty much focused my life on it."

Gray caught himself reflecting on how a man might feel if he were the focus of that much energy and dedication. It would be overwhelming. Quickly he forced his wandering mind back to the guide.

Forming double lines, they tromped inside and began working their way through the wide aisles where dairy cows were tethered. Right away one of the youngsters started sneezing. "Something's tickling my nose."

"It's probably the disinfectant they use to keep the area clean." Garnet produced a tissue from her enormous shoulder bag. "Hold this over your nose if it feels itchy." When it appeared a mini-epidemic had broken out, she dispensed additional tissues.

"I hadn't realized teaching required maternal skills as well," Gray commented.

"Absolutely. In fact, there are times when mothering takes precedence."

She handled both with equal efficiency, another surprise. She wasn't the type of woman a man associated with motherhood. "You were right. Coming here has been a real eye-opener for me."

She looked a little puzzled by the remark, but smiled as if it pleased her. The smile widened when she spied the children flocking to a pair of small black-and-white calves. "Oh, look, Gray. What darling babies."

The guide pointed. "These are one week old, and see, they're wearing name tags too. Can anyone read what they say?"

A noisy clamor of "Michelangelos" and "Raphaels" rang out, prompting Garnet to ask her students to imagine what daring feats ninja calves might perform. The creativity of their responses left Gray smiling and shaking his head. He guessed he could now understand a little better why Garnet said there was never a dull moment around five-year-olds.

They moved on to talk to a dairyman from Brenham. He singled out a tiny girl and called her by name. "Now, Sara," he said, pulling up a three-legged stool. "Next time you get ready to milk a cow, be sure to come at her from the right side. I've had many a cow kick me, and it's always been when I tried to approach her from the left. Think you can remember which side is which?"

Sara giggled and promised she would. Then the whole class laughed hysterically when Miss B sat down and demonstrated her milking technique.

"What's the verdict?" she asked when she'd finally succeeded in getting about a cup's worth in the shiny bucket. "Should I quit my job and move to the farm?"

Childish voices shrieked a resounding "No!" and she stood, dusting her hands together. "I agree."

As they moved along to the next breed of cattle, Gray bent and spoke quietly into her ear. "I want you to stay right where you are, so you're never far away from me."

"That's exactly where I want to be." When she turned the full power of her smile on him like that, he forgot he'd walked away from his office and left behind a situation so volatile, it could explode at any time. For a change, he wanted to think about something other than basketball.

They watched animals being washed with a hose, then their coats were blow-dried and combed and brushed. "Just like at the beauty shop," one child remarked.

"That's right," the FFA guide agreed. "They are

going to be judged later today, and the winner has a chance to make lots of money."

Just then a little boy grabbed Garnet's hand and tugged her to where a two-ton animal stood munching hay. "Man! Miss B, look! What's that cow got between its legs?"

"Jeremy, my jelly roll, that is a bull, not a cow. Which means your question requires a man-to-man answer. Mr. Kincaid will be happy to explain."

As Gray's amusement turned to horror he mouthed the word "Witch." Undaunted, she waggled her fingers and started to amble away. He called after her. "I warned you about your mouth, Miss B. Tonight it's payoff time."

Garnet buttoned a purple brushed-cotton shirt and wrapped a multicolored horizontally striped skirt around her waist. After giving her hair a series of brush strokes, she reached for a wide rawhide belt and cinched it tightly.

Had the past twenty-four hours been so harried that Gray had forgotten about the payoff he'd promised yesterday? She had been so pleased with how he related to her students, she hadn't feared his threat at all. Indeed, she suspected the kind of punishment he had in mind would be thoroughly enjoyable.

But their long, lovely weekend hadn't unfolded as planned. After their return from the Livestock Show, Gray went home to shower and change while Garnet did the same. Friday night, and they were going to dress up and go out on a real date that had nothing to do with basketball or Rodeo.

Her phone had been ringing when she came in the door. According to Gray, all hell had broken loose at his office. He expected to be closeted with Bennett Townsend until the wee hours. He'd sounded so pre-occupied, so grim, her only thought had been to reassure him that she didn't mind.

Yes, she was disappointed because the more time she spent with him, the more she wanted. But she understood that he held a demanding, high-pressure position. It couldn't be easy placating a man who was an acknowledged tyrant. And with the team in a slump following the All-Star game, she imagined the stress had only increased.

He'd finally broken free a few hours ago and had called to say they could try it again Saturday night. Hearing the fatigue and strain in his voice, Garnet suggested they go casual, not plan anything definite. He agreed so readily, she knew he must be exhausted. Right then she made up her mind that he would have a restful and comforting evening.

Minutes later, when she greeted him at the door, she could see that he was beyond exhaustion. "We'll stay home."

"No! I promised you a night out and I've already reneged once."

"That isn't the sort of promise you're bound by when you look like the walking wounded."

He grimaced and rubbed at his bloodshot eyes. "This is one of those times when I feel even worse than I look."

"Want to talk about it?"

"No. Trust me, everything—too much—has already been said. For the next few hours I want to escape.

Forget I ever heard of Bennett Townsend and his Wildcatters and the city of Houston."

"As long as I'm not included in the aforementioned group."

One large hand curved around her neck. "You are most definitely *excluded*." He touched his lips to hers, moved his head from side to side, drew in a breath. "Mmm, this is what I need. You, and lots of . . . you."

"Oh, Gray," Garnet murmured, wrapping her arms around his waist. She parted her lips to receive the full effect of his kiss. But he cut it off.

"We'd better save this for another time. Start now and we'll never get out of here."

"Would that be so bad?"

His index finger trailed from her temple to her jawline, across and down her neck. "I think it would be the best thing I can imagine. But it wouldn't be right, not with me in the condition I'm in right now."

"I understand. I think. So, are you willing to put yourself in my hands for the evening? Do you trust me not to take advantage?"

His red-rimmed eyes closed for a few seconds, then the merest hint of a grin revealed his teeth. "I'm all yours."

The implication was so arousing, Garnet dropped her key ring and barely avoided upsetting a vase of flowers.

She insisted he leave his car in her driveway so they could go in hers. He didn't protest, and soon she had the Cadillac zipping north on the Loop. A small white import cut in front of her and she treated the offender to a deafening blast from her horn. The driver jerked and changed lanes again. "Yee-haw! These air horns I got off a totaled semi spook those little wimps every time."

"Where are you taking me?" he asked, his voice sounding a bit weak. "Providing I live long enough to get there in one piece."

"Someplace you'd never think to go, I suspect. I'm going to see that you are fed and cheered up, and while we're at it, we'll be witnessing the end of an era."

"Uh-oh, I smell trouble. Every time you're in charge of the entertainment, I end up in a pickle."

She laughed, convinced more than ever that his life had been woefully lacking in the zest pickles supplied. "Speaking of which, precisely what did you tell Jeremy yesterday about the bull?"

"Do you really think I'll spill the beans after you put me on the spot that way? No chance. As it is, you know too many of my . . . manly secrets."

She took her eyes off traffic long enough to glance at him with raised brows. "Buttercup, I've barely scratched the surface of your secrets. But I am nothing if not tenacious."

Gray let his head fall back against the headrest. "I haven't put up enough of a fight to notice, have I?"

"Oh, I wouldn't go so far as to say that. You haven't exactly been in hot pursuit the past couple of weeks."

He straightened back up to stare at her. "Hmph. Shows how much you don't know. I've been hot for you since before I knew your name. And to pursue you any harder, I'd have had to camp out on your doorstep. Give me a break, lady."

Garnet's heart swelled and she gripped the steering wheel with both hands. Because she knew they weren't easily given, confessions like that from Gray were worth ten times more than the most glowing compliments from anyone else. She only hoped he wasn't already lamenting his candor.

But he didn't look regretful. In fact, he appeared to be letting go of his earlier tension. He'd laid his head back again and closed his eyes. Good. That was the whole purpose of this evening.

A few minutes later she exited off the North Freeway and followed a stream of traffic to the drive-in theater entrance. Gray stirred, squinted, peered all around. "I don't believe it."

"I thought you'd be thrilled." Garnet paid their admission, chose a row about three quarters of the way back from the screen, and maneuvered the convertible into a space. She hung the speaker on the back window, but left the volume low.

"This is the last drive-in in Houston, and after tonight it's closing for good. That's why I wanted to come, even though it's depressing. I know it doesn't make sense to be emotional about this sort of stuff, but I can't help it."

"You aren't going to cry like you did at the wedding, are you?"

"Nope." She released her seat belt. "I plan to scarf down every kind of junk food the concession shack has while I laugh uproariously at this silly movie."

"And then?"

"Then?" She turned sideways and gave him an exaggerated leer. "Ever fool around in a back seat?"

Seven

"Are you serious?"

"Well, I don't expect names, dates, and places, of course. It was a general question."

"Oh."

"So, have you?"

"Fooled around in a car? No, at least nothing very heavy. By the time my hormones kicked in, I was already too tall. My legs always seemed to be in the way at the crucial moment." He scooted his hips closer to the edge of the seat and angled his left knee toward her.

Garnet watched the action, dry-mouthed. Dressed up, he looked strikingly handsome but just a tad too unattainable. In a rugby shirt, snug-fitting khakis, and casual loafers, he was darned near irresistible. "I see the problem." She ran the seat back as far as it would go.

"On the other hand, I never had a block-long Cadillac to play in." His eyes held humor and a hint of challenge.

She didn't take him up on it. The undercurrent of sexual tension was always present. They could rekindle it anytime with a look, a word, a touch. Right now she thought it was more important to talk. "What did you play, while you were growing up back in Virginia?"

"Basketball. Nothing else interested me. I don't know how it came about, because I sure wasn't steered in that direction. Nobody in my family had ever played, but I always knew that's what I was meant to do. As early as I can remember, I spent hours shooting, dribbling, moving, just handling the ball."

"That's probably why you were so good, so young. Stinky told me you were a sensation in college. All the pro teams wanted you."

In the dusky light she could see his gaze fixed on the big screen, where the concession promo was hawking pizza and popcorn. "Yeah, well, that's in the past. Seems like a hundred years ago."

"Do you sometimes wish you could go back? I imagine things were a lot simpler before you had the kind of pressures and responsibilities that face you every day now."

He stirred and glanced at her. "I don't believe in looking back. Life stands still unless you have the guts to test yourself by setting new goals."

"I can't argue with you there. That's why I love my job so much. Every day it's up to me to make sure each of those minds learns something new." The opening credits of the feature film began to roll. Neither paid them any mind. "Does your current goal coincide with Bennett Townsend's?"

"He and I want the same thing. We're doomed to clash over how to get it." He kneaded at a frown. "How did we end up back on the one subject I swore not to talk about?"

"Probably because you're consumed with it at the moment."

"No. At the moment I am consumed with wanting to make out with a certain luscious-looking redhead." He rested his left arm along the seat back and with the opposite hand reached over to touch her shoulder. "Your side or mine?"

The slight weight set off a sudden burst of longing. She slid across the leather and into his waiting arms. "I really didn't bring you here for this. You know me. I just can't resist teasing."

"Mmm, I know." His breath tickled her ear and made her shiver. "So tease me."

"How?"

"Shouldn't be hard. You shake me up pretty good without even trying."

She turned more fully into him. Her hand shaped the side of his face, her thumb played at the corner of his mouth. "Maybe I'll start here. Think that's safe enough?"

"Try it and see."

His lips were so close, she could almost taste him, almost . . . Her tongue stole out, touched, licked, and then their mouths fused. At once the kiss engulfed her in a storm of sensation, savage but infinitely pleasurable. Her arms stole around his neck, and she abandoned herself to the magic.

The roof of her mouth was so sensitive to Gray's slow stroking that she moaned, a plea for more. When his teeth captured her tongue in a series of soft bites, a sweet ache unfurled deep within her. His hunger was boundless, evoking images of greater intimacy, of joining, sharing, and ultimately, satisfying.

Finally, both gasping for air, they broke apart.

She collapsed against his chest, her breath coming

out in short, uneven pants that matched his erratic heartbeat. "You know the song lyrics, 'A kiss is just a kiss'? Whoever wrote that's never kissed you."

He chuckled. "I might say the same about you. One little taste and I go wild."

"I like you that way." Her index finger trailed across his stomach, outlining one of the stripes on his shirt. "All that control of yours makes me nervous."

"Don't worry. I have almost none around you." A moment passed, rife with anticipation. At last he said, "I won't take it far, but I want to touch you, Garnet. Sometimes I feel like I'm going to fly apart if I have to wait any longer."

"I feel like that too. Touch me."

The hand spanning her waist started to shake, then tightened a fraction. She held her breath, waiting. Slowly, as if he wanted to brand every inch of her, it glided up her rib cage, halted momentarily, then settled over her breast.

Nimble fingers smoothed and lifted and molded her to fill his palm. "Lord, you feel good."

She closed her eyes and her perception heightened. "Good" didn't begin to describe it. Light-headed, delirious, wanton, and much more. Nothing, *nothing*, had ever felt this incredible. She tried to tell him, but all that came out was, "Gray."

"I know. We have to stop, and I will . . . I will, but first . . ." He pressed her back against the seat, lowered his head, and the warm, moist pull of his mouth heated her flesh through the cotton.

"Gray," she repeated, his name the only word she was capable of forming.

His lips traveled upward. "No more. For now." His

voice was as heavy and harsh as his breath on her neck. "Soon, Garnet, I'm going to touch you everywhere. I want you to do the same to me. But in a bed, with plenty of time, and no people sitting ten feet away. And then we'll make love."

She trembled all over, sure she was about to dissolve into a puddle right before his eyes. "Soon," she affirmed, certain that giving herself to Gray had been predetermined the instant she saw him.

Garnet had no fears and no misgivings about the rightness of such a decision. Grammy had told her years ago, "When you meet the man for you, you'll know." Now she had and she did. And being in love was the most wonderful part of all.

They took a few minutes to recover before hitting the snack bar. Loaded down with trays of soft drinks and buttered popcorn, pepperoni pizza and peanuts, plus a sampling of everything else the concession had to offer, Gray said wryly, "The only thing missing is Rolaids."

But he managed to put away more than his share without further complaint. Somehow they never got around to turning up the volume on the speaker. Instead, they spent the entire time trading stories about their childhoods, college years, and adult lives.

For two people with such disparate backgrounds, experiences, and personalities, Garnet kept coming back to the very basic similarities in their philosophies and values. When the movie ended and they were waiting for the traffic to clear, she said, "You might not realize it yet, but in every way that counts, I'm as old-fashioned as you claim to be."

He didn't laugh, which pleased her a great deal. He did, however, tack on a small qualifier. "That, Lady Luck, remains to be seen."

Indeed it did. And Mr. Gray Kincaid was in for the biggest surprise of all.

Once she swung onto the freeway frontage road, Garnet gunned the old Caddy toward the entrance ramp. Right away she saw the colorful lights blinking above them. "Look! It's the blimp. It's been such a perfect night, but I may have to stop and cry over this." She veered into the right-hand lane and braked.

"Seeing the blimp makes you cry?"

"No, I'm crushed because they're taking it away in the spring, to Ohio. That breaks my heart. I've tried every way imaginable to get a ride on it—bidding at auctions, entering contests, outright begging. But my luck hasn't helped there. Now it's leaving and I'll never have another chance." She sniffed.

"It's just an inanimate object. Why do you suppose you're so fond of it?"

"I love it because it makes me happy. Such a friendly, unthreatening thing floating overhead. Reassuring, as if it's letting me know all's right with the world."

He shook his head and pointed a finger at her. "You, Garnet Brindisi, are the most paradoxical woman I've ever met."

Her blue mood vanished. She smiled. "Why, thank you, Gray. I consider that a compliment."

Satisfied that her class was occupied with their art project, Garnet folded herself into a low wooden chair. Teaching, at least the way she did it, wasn't a sit-down job, and she rarely got off her feet during the day. But this was TGIF, last class, time to start winding down.

Outside her open classroom window a mockingbird sang its medley of borrowed songs. She peered into a nearby magnolia tree to see if she could spot it.

In spite of three times the normal rainfall, this had been an unusually mild winter, and spring had arrived early. She picked up a grade book and used it as a fan. The thermometer had climbed to eighty-five degrees, and she was sweltering in her long-sleeved twill blouse, corduroy skirt, and high suede boots. When she got home, the first thing she planned to do was take a shower and put on something cool.

Then she'd begin preparing dinner for Gray. The week had dragged since she'd last seen him on Saturday. They had spoken on the phone several times in the interim, but he'd sounded edgy and distracted. Positive that his anxiety was related to his job and Bennett Townsend, she was going to do her best to get him to confide in her.

Like her brother, Gray kept his problems pent up, never having learned that the mere act of sharing them often inspired a solution. They'd taken a giant first step with their long talk during the movie. Tonight she intended to go one step further.

At this point a declaration of love would be premature. But that needn't stop her from being loyal and supportive of her man.

My man. She liked that. Gray. Mrs. Gray Kincaid.

"Miss B? Miss B? Are you awake?"

Jarred back to reality, she gazed into her student's concerned face. "Oh! Kevin. What was your question?"

"I just wondered if you'd gone to sleep. You looked kinda happy and goofy, like my dog does when he dreams about chasin' rabbits."

"That's exactly right, Kevin. You caught me daydreaming."

Fortunately, only a few minutes remained until time to dismiss school for the week. Once the halls were cleared, she took a few minutes to go over her lesson plans for the next week, then made tracks for the parking lot.

After battling the late Friday afternoon mob at the supermarket, she beat it home, peeled off her sticky clothes, and hopped into the shower. "Ah, blessed relief." But she couldn't dawdle. Gray was due at six-thirty.

Cool at last, she pulled on white silk bikinis and a red cotton knit dress with wide straps, a low neckline, and buttons up the side. She fastened them as far down as her hip and slid her feet into flat sandals. Because she'd be cooking, she bound her hair in a single plait with a series of bands made from seashells.

Ready for the kitchen, and ready for Gray. She checked the time and decided she might as well catch the local news at five while she worked. She had just removed a container of chicken broth from the fridge when the lead story flashed on. "A surprise announcement today from the Wildcatters' front office stunned Houston sports fans!"

Garnet almost dropped the dutch oven. "Gray!"

Staring out at her from the screen, looking composed and remote, Gray spoke into a microphone. While strobes flashed and reporters buzzed, he announced the firing of the team's coach.

With one ear she picked up phrases like "lack of motivation" and "felt we had to take action." All she cared about was the effect this would have on Gray. She knew how much he'd liked and admired the coach. He must have agonized over his role of hatchet man.

"Bennett Townsend, you sorry slug. You're at the bottom of this and Gray's going to wind up taking the rap."

She spun around and marched to the phone. It was then she realized she'd failed to play back the messages on her answering machine. The first was a long-winded computer dating pitch. Next came Gray's, brief and to the point. "I'm sorry I can't make it tonight." A pause. "I'll try to call you soon."

The Wildcatters' number rang busy so she dialed his home number and got a machine. She fiddled with the cord, impatient for the beep. "Gray Kincaid, I will not allow you to hole up and lick your wounds in solitary. I'm making you chicken and dumplings and banana cream pie. If you aren't pulling in my driveway by six-thirty or shortly thereafter, I'll hunt you down." She started to hang up, then added, "P.S. I'm on your side."

Garnet returned to the kitchen and got busy hulling English peas and stirring up the dough for rolled dumplings. She continued watching local news, switching between stations. Gray was taking a beating from the media and the man on the street.

Townsend had never been popular; now they were tarring his hand-picked G.M. with the same brush.

Six-thirty came and went. She wore a path to the front window, peeking out. Nothing. Finally, at five to seven, she saw his lights and sighed with relief. He'd come. The rest was up to her.

She had the door open before he left the car, and the first thing she did was put her arms around him. Along with pleated jeans, loose and faded as she liked them, he was wearing a royal blue cotton sweater. She pressed her mouth to the center of his chest. "Umm, you've just had a shower."

"Trying to drown my sorrows."

She kissed his lips, lightly. "And a drink?"

"More medicine. But the first swallow didn't go down very well, so I gave up on that too."

"I have just the thing." She ushered him into the family room, fussing to get him situated on the plush-cushioned couch. "Here, take these off." She removed his deck shoes and propped his bare feet up on the granite-topped coffee table. Then she bustled into the kitchen and returned with a mug of chamomile tea. "I grew the herbs myself. It's a great de-stressor."

"Garnet, I don't think tea is going to do the trick tonight."

"Drink up and be patient. This is only the beginning." She popped in a long-playing tape of classical music, but kept the volume low. "Close your eyes and let the music transport you."

"What is this? Trying to hypnotize me?"

"Mmm, no. Trying to soothe you." Standing behind the couch, she began to massage his neck and shoulders. "I imagine today has to rank right on up there as one of your all-time worst."

"Not one of. The worst. Period. I feel like a world-class idiot, canning the man who won Coach of the Year only months ago."

"It's been brewing for quite a while, though, hasn't it? This business with Bennett insisting on 'taking action'? That seems to be his favorite phrase."

He waited such a long time, she was afraid he wouldn't reply at all. "Yes. He started harping on the subject on my second day of work here."

"So you've been bucking him for months. That must have gotten tiresome."

"You want the truth? More than once I came this close to telling him to fire us both and be done with the threats. But I thought I could hold it together. I really did."

"I'm sure you tried your best, but with a cow flop like Bennett, there's only so far you can go." Garnet continued to work on him. She was starting to get results. "Were you able to talk with Coach Lindsay, tell him how badly this deal smells? Or did Bennett sit in on the actual firing?"

"No, he was conveniently unavailable."

"Hiding out like the rodent he is."

Gray got out a weak chuckle. "Maybe I ought to sic you on Bennett. Be interesting to see the two of you tangle."

"Anytime. I don't like him a bit better than he likes me. In case you forgot, he has a vendetta against anyone named Brindisi."

"I didn't forget. He's repeated it often enough."

"What?"

"Never mind. It's nothing." He set down his cup,

caught her wrist, guided her around the end of the couch, and tugged her down onto his lap. "You're a good listener. Know that?"

"I aim to please."

"And you do." He looked into her eyes for long, heart-stopping seconds. Then he fitted his mouth to hers.

It was a slow-building kiss with strong undertones of urgency. Garnet parted her lips, taking from him and offering herself, enticing Gray into passion as an outlet for the conflicts raging inside him. This hadn't evolved out of a conscious decision. It stemmed from a very basic feminine need to succor her mate.

His tongue entered her mouth with a surge. She clung to him, threading her fingers through his hair. He made a husky, hungry sound and she absorbed it, twisting to align their upper bodies. With his hands cupping her shoulder blades, he drew her closer . . . rubbing her breasts against his chest.

Garnet shivered uncontrollably as Gray's lips and tongue teased her, alternating gentle caresses with bold, darting invasions. He possesed her mouth, and an echoing vibration thrummed inside her, deep, where he hadn't yet touched.

Restless, she shifted her legs and felt his hand come to rest just below the side opening of her dress. The languorous circular motion of his fingers left a hot imprint on her bare skin. "Been a lot safer if you'd fastened a couple more of these buttons," he said hoarsely.

"Safety is not my main concern tonight." She licked the pad of her ring finger and ran it around the rim of his ear, delighting in his shudder. "Nor is subtlety."

A sudden tension gripped him. "Garnet, I know what you're trying to do here, and I appreciate it. But I'm in a lousy state of mind, and my control is . . . let's just say it won't take me far."

"You're too hung up on control. As for your state of mind, maybe what you need is a temporary escape." She sat up, swung her legs off the couch, and took hold of his hand. "So I guess the real issue is, do you want me?"

His eyes closed and his face contorted as if he were in pain. "That has never been in question."

"Remember what you said about wanting a bed, time, and privacy?" He nodded. "We have all three here." She stood, bringing him up with her.

"You're sure?"

She smoothed away the worry lines on his forehead. "I'm sure enough for both of us."

"Right now I trust you more than I do myself."

Garnet's confidence soared as they walked down the hall to her bedroom, pausing every few steps to exchange kisses and whispered promises. If by some chance her future held more perfect moments than this one, she would surely burst with happiness.

"Oh, Gray, I'm so glad it's you." He looked puzzled and she hastened to add, "Glad you're with me tonight."

"I can't stand the idea of someone else with you like this, tonight or any other time."

She loved the way his eyes widened and a little frown formed, as if the implied possessiveness shocked him. But that was only a small part of what she loved about Gray Kincaid. "You never have to worry about that."

When she opened the door, the only illumination came from her backyard, where Malibu lights nestled among the dense plantings. It seemed brighter because of all the windows and all the . . .

"It's so white," he said, taking in the walls, the high antique brass bed covered in snowy cotton and Battenberg lace and heaped with matching pillows. Even the wood floor was bleached pale.

"Minimizes the heat."

Gray hooked an arm around her waist and pulled her flush with his body. Feet planted wide, he lifted her into the brace of his thighs. "Think it'll have any effect on this?"

He was powerfully aroused and she rode the steady motion of his thrusting hips. "I hope not."

Inch by inch he eased her down until her feet hit the floor. Then he dipped his head and grazed the curve where her shoulder and neck met, his lips tantalizing like the delicate brush of a feather.

Goose bumps dappled her skin and Garnet heard herself moan. Her fingers bunched the knit of his sweater as his mouth skimmed her collarbone, descended to trace the low scoop of her neckline. He left a trail of delicate bites, each one fanning the flame of desire within her.

She was so absorbed, swaying in the throes of his delicious torment, that she was barely aware he had released one of the side buttons, parting the fabric so his hand could find the dip of her waist. He squeezed once, twice, and she made another sound, this one wild and wanton.

Her response seemed to ignite him. His breath came heavier, hotter against her flesh. His hands roamed feverishly now, no longer restrained and not quite gentle. He tore at another button. Undone, it gave him access to her back and midriff, all the way up to the soft undercurve of her breasts.

Straining against him, Garnet knew she was going to scream if he didn't touch her there. She'd waited so long, too long. "All of the buttons, Gray. Hurry."

Fingers unsteady, he undid the top one. There remained only a single button, attaching the strap on that side to the bodice. She guided him to it. When that was freed, she took a step back and lowered her opposite arm. In a graceful wave, the red dress slid to the floor.

Pale eyes swept her from head to toe, and a deep rumble rolled out of his chest. One hand caught her behind the neck, bringing their mouths together as his palm centered on her breast and began a sensual kneading.

After all the waiting, all the anticipation, the rush of excitement was almost more than she could bear. She was too breathless to kiss him and—with his hand working such compelling sorcery—too weak to stand. She sank onto the bed, bringing Gray down beside her. Soft and cool, the coverlet soothed her heated skin.

He urged her to lie back, leaning over her as she reclined against the bank of downy pillows. Garnet was not small, but his hands were so big, they covered her breasts completely.

She watched, had never seen anything so erotic as the rhythmic flex of his fingers . . . until she looked up to see his mouth open and his tongue flicking . . . as if he could taste her.

I have to stop moaning. "I can't stop moaning."

"Don't. I like it."

His mouth replaced his hands, nuzzling, licking, drawing on her until she had to shut her eyes against the sharp ache. "Oh, Gray, I feel all melty."

His hand tracked the curve of her side and hip, to her thigh, then inward where he covered the silk triangle. "Here? Is this where it aches most?"

He knew. "Yes-s-s. And inside."

The heel of his hand pressed gently, rotating. One long finger slipped beneath the elastic and found the heated center of her. Stroked. "Here?"

She moaned for him again, couldn't help herself, couldn't speak . . . undulating, feeling lush and voluptuous, and more womanly than she'd ever dreamed possible.

He had unveiled the most secret and delicate part of her, and at first his caresses were ethereal, arousing her slowly. He murmured incomprehensible words of praise above her ear, into her mouth, against her breast.

An ever-expanding swell was rising inside her, building, demanding. Her neck arched, her hips lifted reflexively, seeking relief from the spiraling hunger, seeking him. "Please. I need you."

"Yes. Soon." In concert with his fingers and their sleek, gliding mastery of her senses, his lips set the boundaries of her world and defined new limits of pleasure. Ravenous, they conquered her mouth. Wide and wet, they worshiped her breasts. And boldly, after he'd skimmed off the final barrier of her clothing, they moved lower to bestow the ultimate intimacy.

"Ahhh." She clutched at his shoulders, begging, "No more." In a single motion she pushed him to his feet and came up onto her knees. "Not until I can touch you too."

Impatient, she stripped the sweater over his head. Seeing him bare-chested for the first time overwhelmed her. "Oh, Gray, you're . . . magnificent." She lavished kisses down his breastbone, over his pectorals, and around his nipples. He shuddered when she daringly used her teeth.

"Finish," he choked out in a voice thick and raw with need. But she fumbled with the button on his jeans and he took over, shucking them off so fast she blinked. If he'd been wearing underwear, it went with the jeans. She blinked again.

"Magnificent," she repeated, "and there's so much of you." One hand encircled him, measuring, stroking. His heat and strength fascinated her. She reveled in the prolonged, lusty groan she drew from him.

"Garnet, you keep that up and I'm not going to last long."

"In that case . . ." She reached over to open the nightstand drawer and removed a box. "I didn't know if you'd come prepared and I was at the store anyway, so I figured, better safe than sorry." She wrinkled her nose. "What a time for a cliché."

"I came prepared," he said, sitting beside her so he could fish in his pocket. "Take down your hair for me."

"It'll be all over the place."

"Yes." He watched as she peeled off each band of shells and tossed them on the floor. Then she shook her head, letting her hair have its way. "Yes."

Seconds later his hands were buried in it and he tumbled her backward, rolling her over, then under him, their legs tangling until he knelt between hers.

In a moment fraught with meaning, he gazed into her eyes, probed lightly to confirm her readiness, and slowly, slowly began to ease himself inside her.

"Gray, this . . . *you* . . . feel so perfect."

But he hadn't penetrated nearly far enough before he felt the resistance and wrenched back as if he'd touched flame. "Oh, God, Garnet. Why didn't you tell me?"

Eight

Gray studied her from the opposite side of the bed. He lay on his stomach, propped up on one elbow. His chest heaved. "Why didn't you tell me?" he repeated.

"I was afraid you'd act just the way you are." She couldn't quite look him in the eye. "And I was afraid you wouldn't want to . . . go through with it."

"Jeez," he said burying his face in a pillow for a few seconds before staring at her again. "I can't finesse this. Give me a chance to think."

"The obvious response to that is, we're past the thinking stage."

"No. This changes things."

"I expected it to. I want it to." She closed the distance between them and walked her fingers up his spine. "Gray, this isn't just an impulse on my part. There hasn't been anyone else because I had never met a man I wanted until you."

At first he resisted her attempt to sway him, but she was generous with her kisses and clever with her hands. He turned on his side and she swirled the tips of her fingers through the damp hair on his chest, over the ridged muscles of his belly, down to the proof that his desire still burned fiercely. "Don't fight it. Don't fight me."

"I can't." He brought her hard against him. "Garnet." Her name a whisper. "I need you too much."

"Take all of me. Now." She twisted sinuously, urging him to cover her, and he was helpless to deny the lure of her body any longer.

Supporting his weight on stiffened arms, he grated, "I'll try to go easy."

He came into her fully, his smooth, supple entry so restrained she felt only a fleeting twinge that presaged the glorious sense of fullness. "Oh, Gray. I didn't know it would feel this . . . wonderful!"

Another whisper, this one a ragged "Yes." And then he began to move.

Garnet wrapped herself around him, surrendering to his silken thrusts, losing herself in the wonder of passionate attunement with the man she loved. She was filled with awareness—the contrasting texture of hard and soft, hushed sounds of shared breathing, their scents blending, enhanced by the heat rising between them.

But those dreamy sentiments soon gave way to a force more primitive and unrelenting. Gray drove into her, all sleek power and controlled strength, pushing her beyond the boundaries of pleasure as she knew it and leading her toward the promise of satisfaction.

Inside her the wondrous agony built, pulsing and pounding until she could no longer contain it. Like a brilliant flash of lightning, it shimmered all around them, an ecstasy so profound that she convulsed and cried out his name, over and over.

Her surrender seemed to galvanize him. The smooth, rhythmic thrusting became less controlled, replaced by a frenzied drive to completion. Love welled up inside her, boundless and immutable. She clung to him, whispering words of praise and reassurance, welcoming the deep, wracking tremors of his release.

Gray had no idea how much time passed before he came back to himself. He heard the clock tick, stirred when Garnet tested the dampness on his back, registered that his full weight was bearing down on her. Reluctantly he started to separate them, but her hands clamped onto his waist.

"Don't go," she said breathlessly.

He didn't have to be told twice. If he had his way, he'd stay right where he was forever, because nothing had ever felt so fine as her tight, clinging warmth. He did lever away so he could see her face. "You okay?"

She sighed and smiled up at him, her beautiful brown eyes soft and unfocused with a satiation that mirrored his own. "Better than okay, but I'm having trouble putting my finger on the proper superlative."

"You're sure I didn't hurt you?" He'd gotten a little carried away at the end. She had that effect on him.

"If you did, I was beyond noticing." She outlined a pattern on his shoulders. "I'd thought about how it would be, the first time. I mean, I'm inexperienced, but not naive. I knew all the mechanics, and what might happen . . . if I was lucky."

Her smile was luminous, and Gray felt as though

he'd died and been reborn. He knew, and yet he needed reassurance. "Were you lucky?"

Her brows climbed. "Was I wrong in assuming a man could tell, could feel, everything?"

He was still inside her, and feeling way too much. Needed some distance. "I'm too heavy. Here, your turn to lean on me." He arranged her alongside him, her head resting on his arm. They stayed that way for a time, silent, exchanging light touches and brief kisses.

But he had to know. "Garnet, my first impression of you was that you were a major-league flirt with more than your share of men. If anyone had told me I would be the first, I'd have said uh-uh, no way. How could I have been so far off the mark?"

"I don't really see myself as a flirt, in the sense of trying to attract men. I'm equally friendly to women, kids, and animals. Early on, I developed a flair for meeting strangers, because we were always on the move. That's the only way I know to relate to people."

"Makes sense, I guess. Still, it's rare for a woman to last until she's your age."

"Well, Maggie Tyler had very definite opinions, and for sixteen years she was a strong influence on my life. Progressive as she was about most things, she didn't put much stock in the new morality."

"As in 'Don't let boys take advantage of you,' and 'Save yourself for marriage'? "

He felt her nod. "If there had been a reason to go against that, I would have. But there wasn't."

"Until tonight. Why now? Why me?"

"Simple. I was attracted to you the first time our

eyes met. I learned to admire your strength and your character. Then I fell in love. How could I not want to make love with you?"

Gray's chest constricted, felt like somebody had stomped on it. His voice sounded croaky when he said, "Love?"

"Yep. Grammy was right. Love is the strongest of all human passions. It hits you in the head, the heart, and the senses, all at the same time."

"I don't know," he said, vaguely aware that his reaction was wrong, yet too dazed to figure out the right one. Garnet in love with him? It was too much to comprehend.

He had always supposed that love grew out of common backgrounds, similar personalities, and shared beliefs. The logical, practical side of him could not concede that it might develop from instant attraction, fascination, and a hard case of lust. Impossible.

An inner voice reminded him of all the women he had known with common backgrounds, similar personalities, and shared beliefs. Several he'd even *tried* to fall in love with. But it hadn't worked, not even with his fiancée. None of them had made him feel a tenth of what he felt for Garnet. Damn! He'd realized up front that she was going to be trouble. What did a man do when he got hooked?

She sat up abruptly and squinted at the clock. "Almost nine! What a terrible hostess I am. Promised you dinner and instead I—"

"Gave me exactly what I needed." It was the truth. It was also a lie. Her declaration of love had given him more than he needed.

She stretched to plant a thorough kiss on his lips.

"I'm glad. But you must be starving. With everything you had going on, I'll bet you didn't eat all day. I'll have a meal on the table in twenty minutes."

Crawling from the bed, she scooped up her discarded red dress and held it at arm's length. The shadowy light gilded her body; his own surprised him by stirring vigorously.

"Garnet, that is one sexy number. Put it back on and I can pretty well guarantee you won't make it to the kitchen."

She glanced down, saw his erection, and her eyes gleamed. "Hmm. Maybe I'd better feed you first and save the dress for later."

After urging him to stay put, she made a trip to the adjoining bathroom. Then, dressed in loose slacks and an oversized shirt, she left him alone. Taking his time, Gray ambled to the bath, intent on a quick shower. He hit the switch and looked at his reflection in the mirrored wall.

"Sweet Lord," he swore, leaning on the edge of the counter for support. Like some ancient, savage warrior, he bore the traces of Garnet's virginity, a ritualistic badge.

The visible proof that he had been her first lover filled Gray with a ferocious, barbaric satisfaction that both shocked and disgusted him. He didn't see himself as the type of man to glory in such an archaic rite of initiation and possession. But all during his shower and as he dressed, the satisfaction lingered.

He still had no clear-cut idea of what lay ahead for them. Nor could he put a label on his feelings for her. It didn't matter. He'd made her his woman and there was no backing off from that.

• • •

"I don't know your middle name."

"Should that be a requirement for what we've been doing?"

Garnet giggled. "Probably. You did get awfully familiar."

"Mmm. Let's not forget who did the encouraging."

"Mmm." She'd whipped together a meal and he had devoured every bite. Then she had announced her intention to soak in the tub and he'd generously offered to help. One thing led to another and, after Gray had given her a breathtakingly informative lesson on the versatility of soap and water, they'd ended up back in her bed.

"I don't know yours either, you know."

"Honey chile, with two like Garnet and Brindisi, what do I need with another? I'm an N-M-N, no middle name." She let out an extended sigh and arched into his inflaming touch. "Come on, give."

"Grayson."

"Ah. And your first?"

"William."

She ran through his whole name silently, deciding it sounded very straitlaced, very upper-drawer. But he was naked and more than a little turned on, and his thumb and index finger were playing wicked games with her nipple. A William Grayson wouldn't be that uninhibited.

"So, Billy Gray, you lookin' to score a triple double?"

He chuckled at her basketball analogy, sent his fingers on a daring new mission of discovery, and said, "Yeah, Garnet N-M-N, I'm lookin' to score."

• • •

Garnet woke alone in tangled sheets, alarmed for a few seconds because she feared Gray had deserted her. Then she saw his shoes and smiled. Just before she'd drifted off, she had asked him to stay. He'd kept his promise.

She sank back to her pillow and lazed dreamily for a while longer, wanting to savor each memory from the previous night. But why dwell on memories when the man she'd made them with was nearby? She scrambled up, winced, and sat back down. Gray had tried to warn her that she'd be sorry today for last night's overindulgence. She didn't regret a thing, would do it again, given the chance.

Which was not likely. Gray was embroiled in a crisis that had barely begun. She understood that claimed first rights, cursing Bennett all the while for his rotten timing.

Walking gingerly, she went to the closet and searched for a robe that would make a better impression than the tatty old Royal Stewart plaid she'd worn for years.

She settled on a terry-lined rose floral print, did her teeth, and dragged a brush through her hair so she could get it pulled back and tied with a scarf. Not great, but presentable enough to make an appearance.

Gray was sitting at the breakfast table, a glass of juice and the unopened newspaper in front of him. His jeans were rumpled from being chucked to the floor too many times, and the sweater hadn't fared much better.

He looked so tired that Garnet immediately felt guilty for crashing shortly after midnight and sleeping straight through until seven. "Did you get any rest at all?"

"Some. I had a lot on my mind."

She took a homemade coffee cake from the freezer and popped it into the microwave to defrost. "I had hoped you could forget about Bennett, if only for a little while."

"I did put him on hold." He made wet circles on the tabletop with his glass. "Thinking about us and our . . . predicament kept me awake."

Predicament? That sounded ominous. She sat across from him and reached for his hand. "Didn't we resolve this last night?"

"No. Last night complicated things to the point that I had to make a decision."

"A decision?" *Please don't say it was a mistake.*

"Yes. I think we should get married."

Incredulous, she shot out of the chair. "What? Married?" Of all the possibilities she might have considered, this one didn't even make the list.

He had to be joking. And she would tease him back. They'd both laugh. "I doubt there's a chance I'm pregnant. You were very careful about eliminating the risk."

Cool, sophisticated Gray Kincaid blushed. "I'm not worried about that."

"Then I must be missing something important here."

He concentrated on her apple-for-the-teacher collection arranged on the glass shelves of her greenhouse window. "You were a virgin, Garnet. That's something any decent man should respect and honor."

Southern gentleman. "You mean you feel obligated to marry me because you . . . ?" It was inconceivable, a scenario out of a nineteenth-century novel. "What a charmingly outdated notion of chivalry."

"I'm no knight in shining armor, obviously. I didn't love you from afar. This has nothing to do with chivalry."

"Tell me what it does have to do with. Don't hide your feelings from me."

"It isn't about feelings, either."

"That's what I was afraid of."

"It's about doing the right thing."

How could he make the right thing, the thing she wanted most, sound so wrong? His calculated, emotionless statement left her queasy. "When you were engaged before . . . was it because something like this happened?"

Fingers drumming, he stared at his glass. Garnet figured he deemed the question too personal. She didn't care. It was important that she learn the truth. No," he said at last. "The circumstances were entirely different. She wasn't, uh . . . you were a first for me."

That news filled her with perverse pride. "Honor is high on the list of traits I admire, Gray. But it's not a good enough reason for marriage. Much as I appreciate the offer, I can't say yes."

Elbow on the table, palm to forehead, he was a study in frustration. "Garnet, my life is about as messed up as it can get right now. Don't fight me on this. Please."

Her heart went out to him. She hurried to stand behind his chair and twined her arms across his chest. "You mustn't think of it as me fighting you. In fact, you need to put it out of your mind for the time being."

"I can't. We have to make plans before I leave, because as soon as I show my face, the vultures are going to be lying in wait to pick my bones. It'll be a miracle if there's anything left. Yesterday was just the opening shot. They'll have recovered from the shock by today and be in the mood for some serious carnage."

Her arms tightened; she kissed the back of his neck. "Which is why you shouldn't get distracted by what happened last night." She laughed. Nipped his earlobe. "Well, it's permissible to get a little distracted about how fantastic it was."

He stiffened and evaded her mouth. "Garnet." Her name a warning.

"All I'm trying to say is don't get hung up on mapping out our entire future this morning. We've plenty of time for that. Let's focus our combined attention on tossing the gators out of the pirogue. Then we can drain the swamp."

"Huh?"

"Uncle Irvin. What he meant was, you have to first battle the most immediate threat. Once that's eliminated, you can carry on with your original objective."

"Do you have a relative and an adage to fit every occasion?"

"What can I say? I come from a long line of folk philosophers."

•　•　•

Gray slouched in his chair and watched the flurry of activity in the kitchen. She had insisted on fixing him breakfast, and like everything else she did, Garnet cooked with dash and fervor. Eggshells arced into the sink, her version of a set shot. French toast and plump little sausages sputtered on a griddle, and she wielded two spatulas like a marimba player, while singing loudly in Spanish.

He couldn't care less about eating, but try convincing her. She was positive a big helping of "comfort food" would cure whatever ailed him.

He didn't really buy that, yet his inclination was to trust her. Somehow she seemed to know what was best for him. No matter how much guilt plagued him this morning, he would never regret last night. Before getting home and playing her message, all he'd wanted was solitude. After he heard her voice, it was as if some of the oppression evaporated, and he couldn't run to her fast enough.

What a change she had wrought in his life. She'd hit him with a number of surprise blows and, in the process, contradicted almost every opinion he had formed of her at their first meeting. In only three weeks he'd gone from vowing that he had no interest in her to proposing.

Actually, he conceded, squirming uncomfortably, he'd botched the proposal. Beneath her rash, brash exterior, Garnet was amazingly soft and sentimental. The type who'd have a weakness for romantic gestures and pretty words.

Too bad. Gray was the wrong guy to provide those frills. She would have to make do with his honorable intentions. But she'd tossed those back in his face too, however graciously. Said she couldn't marry him. Not wouldn't, couldn't. What kind of argument was that?

Logically, he knew he ought to take her advice and drop the subject. From all indications she was feeling blissfully content—not compromised—as a result of their lovemaking. He'd done his duty as a gentleman. Now he was off the hook.

But the idea of marrying her just kept looping through his brain. Some instinct he didn't begin to understand compelled him to pin Garnet down, get a commitment from her. He strongly suspected it had nothing to do with integrity.

Oblivious to him, she waltzed a platter around the open oven door. In spite of everything weighing him down, he smiled. She had that effect on him. And she said she loved him. If so, shouldn't he be able to convince her to see things his way?

Love. Damn! What was he going to do about that?

Gray slid the paper out of its waterproof plastic, spread it flat, and scanned the front-page article on yesterday's debacle. It was a reasonably straightforward report of what had happened . . . up to a point. Only he and Bennett knew the full story. For varying reasons, neither of them would ever reveal everything that had led up to the firing.

It was in the sports section that he'd be crucified, but some masochistic urge dictated he read every negative word. Predictable, the rational part of him acknowledged. In reality the condemnation felt like acid eating away at his dreams. His past experience hadn't included coping with bad press. Now he was in for a trial by fire.

"Oh, shoot." Garnet whisked the paper aside. "That isn't the kind of tripe you ought to read before breakfast. It'll ruin your appetite."

She was bound to be disappointed if she expected him to eat four slices of French toast and the pound or so of sausage she'd heaped onto his plate. "All I really wanted was the juice."

"Nonsense!" She hustled back to the kitchen and returned with a small pitcher. "Maple syrup. The real thing from Vermont, not that watered-down, flavored junk." She stuck her arm out and drizzled some of the syrup onto his plate, then doused her own thick slices of bread. "Now give me a condensed outline of the damage, so we'll know what we're up against."

She sounded combat-ready, as if it were the two of them against the world. "Robert Falcon," he said, naming his personal choice of a broadcaster and daily columnist, "thinks the firing squad was a way to appease discontented fans. You can't ax every player, so get rid of the coach and that's supposed to send a message that the team's okay." Gray picked up his fork. "He gives it a ten for shock value, and a two, maybe three, for effectiveness."

"Awright! Falcon looks and sounds like a wienie, but he's got my vote for smarts." She forked up a piece of dripping toast. "What's Mr. Malt-O-Meal, Henry Kant, have to say?"

Gray sawed a sausage link in half, then impaled it. "Clichés like 'Chemistry is the advantage. We need so many shooters, rebounders, and defensive players. A balance of talent, where everybody understands his role and plays toward a common goal.' Hit on the magic combination and we'll have a winner."

She faked a yawn. "So original. But then, that man's entire vocabulary consists of platitudes." She took another hit of syrup. "What about Stinky? I can't imagine him adding anything that might smack of the perceptive."

"You know Stinky. Never at a loss for words. Essentially, he's calling for me to be ridden out of town on the same rail as Bennett Townsend. That's after I've been publicly dismissed and subjected to ridicule."

"Let me look at it," she said, snatching the paper. She plowed through Stinky's commentary at speed-reading pace. Her eyes narrowed in direct proportion to her pursing lips until her face was wrinkled up like a prune. "Oooh, that chicken-livered, yellow-bellied, cement-headed turkey buzzard. Who does he think he is, anyway?"

"He's only written what a lot of people are thinking," Gray pointed out, knowing he would have to remain impassive in order to survive. "Fact is, I can't expect to win any popularity contests over this deal."

"Ken Overton may be quoting straight from the Gospel, but he isn't going to attack you and come out unscathed. Wait till I get hold of that slimy little piece of worm dirt. They'll be dragging Buffalo Bayou with a tea strainer to find the pieces." Her eyes crackled with electricity, her face was flushed, and one fist punched the air.

"Garnet, their business is selling papers, and every reporter lives for a controversy of this magnitude. Media flaps go with the territory. I can't take it personally."

"Well, I can. When they're persecuting you, I can take it *very* personally." She flung the paper with Stinky's front-page article to the floor, scrambled out of her chair, and ground first one foot, then the other, into his small picture. "Mess with us, you fork-tongued smut slinger, and I'll stick your gizzard full of pin holes."

"Simmer down," Gray said, smiling at her vehemence. She had worked up quite a lather, and she was spectacular in her outrage. "I think it's going to take more than voodoo to silence Stinky."

"What voodoo? I'm throwing a temper tantrum, and I've barely warmed up." She pulled out the chair nearest him and sat down, leaning forward as if to divulge a secret. "How's this for revenge? I'll start by burning his shoe lifts." She giggled. "Then, fly his hairpiece from one of those Summit flagpoles. Oh, and I'll take out an ad . . . no, no, a billboard, one of those big suckers in 3-D."

He captured her wildly gesturing hand. "Even if I were the vindictive sort, revenge is not my top priority at the moment. There's a simpler way to handle the problem."

"Good point. Why not take out a contract on him? It's common knowledge that in Texas you can get dirty deeds done dirt cheap. While I'm at it, I'll include Bennett. Maybe get a price break for two."

Gray drew back slightly, undecided whether he ought to laugh or be appalled. "I will assume you are joking."

"I'll have to give it some more thought before I can say for sure." She crossed her arms, and her mouth formed a pout. "I still think those two weasels need to be taught a lesson, and I'm mad enough to take both of them on."

He had to call a halt to this absurd conversation. But Garnet's unwavering loyalty was like nothing he'd ever witnessed before. Most women would have hedged their bets, tried to second guess which side would come out on top.

She had lined up on *his* side, no questions asked, ready—no, eager—to fight in his defense. No man had a right to expect more. Most men had to settle for a whole lot less.

He stood, and she rose with him. "Sooner or later, I'll have to face the music. I think it's time."

"I know, and I understand." She glanced away, and when her eyes came back to his, they were misty with unshed tears. "I love you, Gray. Whatever happens in the next few days or weeks, I hope that means something to you."

His gut burned, and his throat. Even his eyes. But deep inside, he ached. A little too roughly, he pulled her against him. Soft and pliant, she yielded. His hands gentled.

She'd given him so much—love and support—and he'd soaked it up. But he felt inept and worthless that he couldn't give her something as special in return. No matter how he looked at it, the score was lopsided, and he didn't know how to even it up. "I don't want to leave, Garnet."

"Remember I'm here. For whatever you need."

He searched for words that eluded him. Finally he just joined their lips in a kiss that he hoped would be enough for the time being. And then he had to get out of there before he made a complete fool of himself.

Nine

Garnet maintained a cheerful front, smiling and waving at Gray as he backed out of her driveway and disappeared down the street. Once she'd closed the door, her effervescence went up in smoke. It wasn't so much depression that afflicted her, but rather an overpowering sense of helplessness.

She wanted to stand side by side with Gray throughout his ordeal, as if her presence could provide a buffer against the abuse heaped upon him. That was out of the question. This was his job, his responsibility, and he'd want to deal with it alone. He had operated as a solo act for so long, he wouldn't think about looking to anyone else for help.

There wasn't a doubt in her mind that he could weather the storm of media and fan censure. Gray was mature, confident, and disciplined, and he possessed an inner core of toughness that would see him through the upcoming weeks. Bennett, however, would try Job's patience. He would be a habitual thorn in Gray's side. When the current strife died down, he'd stir up some more, as he'd been doing for most of the twenty years since he had brought the team to Houston.

Bennett Townsend was a pugnacious pain-in-the-butt, and she'd like nothing better than to eradicate him. The memory of her threat to take out a contract on him made her grin. Gray clearly hadn't known whether to take her seriously or not. The hit man idea had been a symbolic show of bravado, of course. But what if there was some legitimate means of removing Townsend from the picture?

She began to meander through the house, picking up random objects, examining them without really seeing. It was a way of marshaling her thoughts and pondering options. It took nearly an hour before a viable solution emerged and sent her scurrying to the phone.

If she was lucky enough to get this particular ball rolling, she could at least assist Gray from the sidelines. And in her own small way, she'd also be doing the whole city a favor.

"Hello, Mrs. It's Garnet. Is Dewdaddy home?"

She listened patiently to a rambling discourse, finally learning that Dewey Whitt was available. He picked up another phone and said, "How's my girl? Ready to fleece me at the poker table again?"

"No, I'm not calling about our poker game. I need to talk to you about something more important."

He told her to come right over, so she hurriedly showered, dressed, and revved up her car for the short drive to the Whitts. Unable to curb her eagerness, she hummed one of her students' favorite songs. It filled her with optimism.

Garnet was not rich or powerful, but she knew folks who were. Dewdaddy had bought up huge tracts of land in the outlying areas when it was worth almost nothing. Later, during the boom times of rampant building and expansion, he'd sold or developed it himself, amassing a fortune in the process.

Though he lived modestly and kept a notoriously low profile, very few business deals went down in Houston that Dewey Whitt didn't know about. Crossing her fingers that he was in the pipeline on this one too, she rang the doorbell.

"Don't you look pretty this morning," Mrs. said, standing on tiptoe to kiss Garnet's cheek.

A little burst of heat spread over Garnet's skin as she stammered "Thank you." Had making love with Gray altered her appearance? It had definitely affected how she felt, but she'd assumed the change was an internal one. "I'm sorry to barge in on such short notice."

"Don't be silly. You've been like one of ours since you were six. You must always think of this as your second home. Now go right in. Dew's waiting in his study."

"Hey, darlin'," he greeted her when she peeked in the open doorway. "What's got you so fired up this morning?"

Garnet claimed one of the ancient, soft leather chairs. "You remember meeting Gray Kincaid at the kickoff dance?"

"Indeed I do. As soon as we got out of earshot, Mrs. told me you'd finally hooked up with a man worthy of you." He scratched his head. "Can't rightly say how she figured that out so quick, but I know better 'n to argue with Mrs."

"Good thing you didn't, because she hit the mark dead on. I'm in love with Gray."

"Well, that _is_ news." He seemed to be examining her for outward signs, and again she felt the flush of memories. "Naturally, we'll want a chance to get to know him better. What with your grandparents gone and your daddy an absentee, I kinda feel it's my responsibility to make sure his intentions are honorable."

Garnet smiled at the old-fashioned attitude and refrained from mentioning that she'd been looking after herself for several years. "Dewdaddy, even you would be impressed with the man's honor. Trust me, I speak from experience. You might say it's my reason for being here."

"I'm listening," he said, picking up on the gravity in her tone.

"Like everyone else in town, you must have heard what happened with the Wildcatters on Friday." He inclined his head a bit and she continued. "Bennett Townsend's been pestering Gray all season about getting rid of the coach, but Gray had managed to divert him until the 'Cats lost big on Thursday night to the worst team in the league. That was the last straw. Somebody's head had to roll."

"A professional team, like any other big business, exists to make a profit. Winning translates into ticket sales and sponsors' revenue. That's the bottom line."

"I understand how it works, which is not to say I agree with the ideology. But my interest is based on strictly personal and purely selfish motives. You see, Gray can't devote much of his time or attention to our relationship as long as Bennett is the big boss."

Dewdaddy's expression turned black, a rare occurrence. Shaking his head, he observed her with one eye closed. "Townsend . . . I reckon he knows about you."

"I met him once, and a nastier man I never hope to encounter. He was downright rude."

"So he figured out who you are?"

"He made the connection between me and my father. Told me to give Lucky a message and didn't bother to disguise the threat. I've wondered and wondered what that was about. Is it possible he thinks Lucky cheated him in a card game? That's the only link, however tenuous, I've been able to come up with."

Head still shaking, Dewey Whitt, averted his eyes. "After all these years, this is the damndest coincidence. Stranger than fiction, for sure."

Garnet sat forward. "What do you mean?"

"How old is Ty now?"

"Thirty-two. What does that have to do with any of this?"

"About ten months before Ty was born, your grandparents, Mrs., and I took your mama and our Elena to celebrate New Year's in Las Vegas. The girls were just eighteen, in their first year of college. To make a long story short, Anna saw Lucky Brindisi at a blackjack table and fell in love at first sight."

"She's told me the story many times. And about how he followed her back here and talked her into eloping."

"Yes, but I'll wager she didn't tell you she was keeping company with another young man at the time. Lots of us thought it was serious, and the man apparently did too. But Lucky just spirited her away right from under his nose, and there wasn't a thing anybody could do to change her mind. I'd say Anna's never looked back."

Garnet swallowed, wary, yet too curious not to pursue the story's end. "I still don't get the connection. Unless . . . no, the man couldn't have been Bennett. That's too weird."

"It's weird, all right. But true. According to gossip, Lucky challenged Townsend to a card game. Swore he'd bow out of the picture if he lost. Well, you can imagine the outcome there. And no, Bennett never accused Lucky of cheating. That didn't stop him from being furious, however. Told Lucky to get out of town and never come back. Far as I know, the threat's still in effect."

"Good heavens," Garnet breathed. "No wonder hearing my name gave him apoplexy. Still, I can't imagine anyone holding a grudge for over thirty years."

"Neither can I, but it sounds as though Townsend's an expert at it." Each of them reflected on the tale for a few moments until Dewdaddy said, "We got sidetracked. What kind of help do you need from me?"

She fitted her hands together and took a deep breath. "Every so often a rumor circulates that a group of investors is negotiating to buy the Wildcatters. The sale never comes off and most people think it's a ruse of Bennett's to whip up interest in a sale."

"I wouldn't put it past him."

"Nor would I. But the report crops up a little too often to discredit. Could you put out some feelers and see if there really is a potential deal in the works, and what the status of it is now?"

Dewdaddy chuckled. "Want to buy your man a team?"

"Sure, Bennett's asking only a hundred million." Which she would gladly pay if she had it. "I'd be content just to see Gray get a chance to do his job with a minimum of interference. And I don't think that's going to happen as long as Bennett pulls the strings."

"Let me make a few calls, look into it. I'll get back to you as soon as I have anything solid."

"Thanks, Dewdaddy," she said, walking around the desk to drop a kiss on his cheek. "I owe you one."

"Keep that in mind the next time we play poker. Speaking of which, I got something going that might interest you. Let me take you and Mrs. to lunch and I'll fill you in on the details."

The media buzz continued into the new week, and Garnet had to settle for a couple of perfunctory phone calls from Gray, usually late at night. As she had expected, he'd taken control and was bringing everything back in line. He had held a clear-the-air meeting with the players and assistant coaches, participated in practices, and reclaimed a small degree of support because the 'Cats had won three consecutive games since the firing.

Garnet had determined that she could best help him by being a good listener and sounding board, and she was thankful he trusted her enough to confide. While his obligations loomed large, she had put her own on hold, but they hadn't ceased to exist.

Dewdaddy had offered her a golden opportunity, one she couldn't afford to pass up.

She wanted to discuss it with Gray, but never got the chance. He'd been traveling on all the road trips. As soon as he returned he was submerged in administrative details.

When they were well into a second week and he still hadn't found time to break away, Garnet decided she couldn't wait any longer. After school on Thursday she slipped into a practice session at the Summit, hoping to waylay him.

Not only was he there, but he was on the floor, working out with the team. To remain inconspicuous, she chose a seat fairly high up and behind some other spectators. For thirty minutes longer they ran drills and plays, but she watched only Gray. And when the newly named interim coach blew a whistle, they disbanded, gathered up armfuls of gear, and struck out for the locker room. All except Gray. He never stopped.

One by one the remaining audience drifted away until only the two of them were left in the huge arena. Mesmerized, she sat unmoving, barely breathing.

He streaked the length of the court, did a three-sixty turn, and dunked the ball. Leaping to catch the high bounce in midair, he did a reverse dunk. Zigzagging, stopping short, changing directions, he dribbled the ball back to midcourt. Then he turned and charged, leaving his feet at the top of the key, soaring to the basket, finger-rolling the ball in as gently as one would arrange an orchid.

Garnet's breath backed up in her chest, her heart beat in a heavy cadence. She couldn't sit still. Gray moved with the grace of a ballet master and the stamina of a superb racehorse, every muscle defined and working at its peak. His brief shorts were drenched, sweat dripped from his hair, the bare skin of his chest and back glistened.

Seeing him like this aroused her on a very primal level. He had never looked better, and she had never wanted him more.

She lost all sense of time until he simply stopped, stood immobile for a few seconds, then bent and put his hands on his knees. Silently, she descended the steps to courtside. She clapped, three times slowly, and said, "That was beautiful."

He straightened and pivoted, searching. When their eyes met, his were distant and slow to focus, as if he were returning from a trance. "Garnet?"

"Yep." Her voice sounded about as unsteady as her legs felt. "Thought maybe you forgot what I looked like."

That brought him back to reality and off the court. "Hardly. I just didn't expect to see you here."

"I called and found out you had open practice this afternoon, so I figured it was all right to show up."

He paused in the act of toweling his face. "Is something wrong?"

"Well, no. I wanted to let you know I'll be out of town over the weekend, in case you tried to reach me." That sounded petulant. She tried for a lighter tone. "We're leaving after school tomorrow. Monday's a holiday so we won't be back until that night."

"Who's we? And where are we going?"

"Dewdaddy and Mrs. plus a couple of their friends. Several times a year they go to Vegas to meet people they know from all over. This time they asked me to go along."

He looped the towel around his neck and crossed his arms. "I guess I don't need to ask if poker is involved."

She decided to leave out the fact that Dewdaddy was bankrolling her in a round of high-stakes games with some of the best players in the country. "I'll be playing, yes. It's a perfect setup to get significant bucks into the college fund. Who knows, if I'm real lucky I might win enough for us to double the number of scholarships we can give next year."

"Didn't anything I said to you the other night sink in?"

"Everything you said sunk in." Knowing how testy Gray was about her gambling, why had she chosen to confront him directly? *Because you can't give up trying to reason with him.* "I thought we agreed to disagree on this subject."

"No, that was your solution. I didn't agree and I haven't changed my mind." He shook his head in disgust. "A friendly game in somebody's living room, maybe I can understand that. But, Garnet, Vegas is another story. Everything crass and corrupt in human nature is magnified tenfold."

"I don't care a fig for Vegas. I'm going for one purpose, and you know it's important."

"There are a lot of unsavory characters out there. You'll have to watch yourself."

"For Pete's sake, Gray, I'm not going to be hanging around any lowlifes."

"All the same, we both know how you attract . . . people. Some of them might get ideas."

"Surely you're not jealous."

"No, dammit." He scrubbed his face again. "I don't know. Maybe I am, a little. It's obvious you haven't been getting a whole lot of anything but trouble from me. Some smooth operator out there could take one look at you and decide to sweep you off your feet."

"Things like that don't happen when you're in love." But, Garnet reminded herself, he didn't know that, because he wasn't in love. Or if he was, he'd kept it a secret.

He tipped her chin up. His eyes were the color of a frozen lake; heat poured off him like a furnace. "What if I don't want you to go? Suppose I ask you to stay away from there, to not gamble at all?"

"I hope you won't do that, Gray. You'll only make it more difficult for both of us." She grasped his wrist. "We haven't seen each other in almost two weeks. If we can only steal a few minutes, let's not spend them bickering. Could you kiss me instead?"

He hesitated, as though he might refuse. Garnet's emotional state was so fragile, she wavered between bursting into tears and slugging him.

He relieved her of the decision, catching her under the arms and molding her body to his. His mouth was as hot as the rest of him, and as wet, taking hers in a blaze of passion and possessiveness.

As always, one taste of him ignited her senses and sent her soaring. She twisted to get closer; her palms flowed over the slippery skin of his shoulders and back. His restless hands took even bolder liberties, moving between them, touching where she was most receptive, exciting her with brazen familiarity.

"You make me crazy," he groaned in a voice that

evoked images of coarse sandpaper. "I want you here, now, and that makes me even crazier."

"I know exactly how you feel. And I'm almost reckless enough to cheer you on."

He grimaced and eased her away from him. "During the day, I can't let myself think about us. There's too much going on. But when I'm alone, Garnet, I can't get you out of my mind. I keep replaying the night we spent together, feeling like a heel because I've deserted you, and how you must be thinking I used you for a one-night stand."

"Of course I don't think that! I don't even think you'd be capable of such a thing." She lay her hand on his arm, comforting. "I told you to take the pressure off yourself where we're concerned. I've waited twenty-six years for you. I'm not going anywhere."

"Except Vegas."

"That's right." She took a moment to reconsider, then made a huge concession to love. "Unless you want me to be with you over the weekend. I mean really *with* you, not standing by the phone hoping you'll have time to call."

He rubbed his knuckles along his jawline. "I can't. We're catching a plane in three hours. Have a game tomorrow night in Salt Lake. On Saturday afternoon I'm checking out a college prospect at Brigham Young, and Sunday we play in San Diego."

"Then there's no reason for me to change my plans."

Gray gazed into her eyes so intently, she could feel the force of his will pulling at her, attempting to use her love to compel her to do his bidding. "If you feel you have no choice, how can I stop you?"

"It's something I have to do." Each knew where the other stood, and there was no point in prolonging the friction. What they needed was a bit of remedial playfulness. "Three hours, huh?" She winked. "How 'bout a quickie, here on the floor of the Summit?"

He didn't get into the spirit of her jest. "That's all I need at this point, to give Townsend more ammunition."

"Bennett! Wait till you hear this. I've found out the most extraordinary thing about him." She related Dewdaddy's story about the triangle involving her parents and Bennett. "Now we know why he took an instant dislike to me."

"Yeah, I guess that explains it." He didn't appear relieved to hear the reason. "But knowing what motivates him doesn't change anything."

Reading between the lines, Garnet came up with an odious possibility. "Oh, Gray, is he giving you a hard time because you're seeing me?" Bennett Townsend was capable of vindictiveness over less.

"Nothing I can't live with."

Spoken like a true stoic. "I'm sorry he's dumping this on you, along with everything else. What are you telling him?"

"About us? Not a word. It's none of his business."

Maybe not, but that wouldn't stop Bennett. He'd have plenty to say about Gray consorting with a Brindisi, might even threaten him with the loss of his job. Gray didn't need any more burdens, and the fact that she was indirectly responsible for this one made her resent Bennett even more. "Hang in there. I'm working on the ultimate solution."

•   •   •

Garnet gazed out her window at the Strip, remembering Gray's assessment of Las Vegas. He'd been right that much of it was tawdry and crass, and she'd seen too many people approach the games with desperation in their eyes. The veneer of respectability on gambling was quite thin.

Gray worried needlessly about the risk of her being addicted. If he had even an inkling of how deplorable she found this lifestyle, he'd have no more cause for concern. Nothing short of a powerful motivation could lure her here, and she was ecstatic with the two thousand she'd won today. But after only one night and day, she couldn't wait to get back to Houston.

How had her mother tolerated living like this for so many years? Hotel rooms, no matter how sumptuous, did not take the place of a home. She'd done it for love of Lucky, and Garnet was sure Anna had no regrets. Now that she'd fallen in love, too, Garnet understood a little better the sacrifices a woman might be tempted to make.

She had offered to forego the trip here to be with Gray. Ultimately, if she were forced to choose between him and the dream of helping all those who asked for it, would she pay the high price for love?

Uncomfortable with the direction of her thoughts, she turned back to face the room. Dewdaddy made several trips here every year, and he was obviously considered a "whale," a high roller in casino lingo. They'd been met by a limo at the airport and greeted by a casino host upon arrival. The complimentary suites were another sign that management was happy to accommodate him and his party.

This hotel was tasteful by local standards, though

not without its share of theatrical flourishes. Like the huge sunken tub with gold-plated seahorse faucets. And the enormous platform bed with three wide carpeted steps leading up to it, and overhead drapings befitting a sheik's tent.

She climbed the steps and flung herself atop the gold brocade coverlet. Rolling over and over, like a dolphin in water, she allowed free rein to a fantasy involving her and Gray and this great, ostentatious bed. That brought on a fit of giggles so unrestrained, she barely heard the knock on her door.

Hurrying through the parlor, she checked her watch. The Whitts were here early to pick her up for dinner and she was dressed only in her robe. She opened the door. "Look at—" It wasn't Dewdaddy and Mrs. She closed her eyes, shook her head, and opened them again. Still there. Still tall. Looking beat but wonderful. "Gray?"

"Did you forget what I looked like?"

She'd asked him something similar two days ago. "Hardly. I'm just having trouble believing you aren't a figment of my fantasy."

"I'm real. Touch me and see." He took her hand and placed it over his heart. It was thumping as madly as her own.

"What about all the other things you were supposed to do? How did you get here? Why did you come?"

"The last question is the only one that counts. Because I couldn't stand not being with you another day."

"That's good enough for me." Keeping her hand where it was, she used the other to draw him into the room. When she spied a leather suitcase in the hall, her pulse, which had begun to slow, kicked up again. "I hope that luggage means you can stay."

"Until late tomorrow morning." He reached out to retrieve the case and shut the door. Then he kissed her, pouring into it a wealth of longing and the promise of passion, a promise she gave back with fervor.

Against his mouth, she said, "Let me have a second to phone Dewdaddy and Mrs. and tell them not to count on me for dinner or the show. My plans for the evening have just changed."

"I've already talked to Mrs. Whitt. Called hotels from the airport until I found them. She said we 'children' should spend the time together and not worry about them."

"Well, then. What are we waiting for? Let's see, I think we left off right about here." She nibbled on his lower lip as a prelude to resuming the kiss, but Gray leaned back.

"Don't tempt me." He walked over and dropped onto the couch, as if distance were imperative. "We ought to go out, do the town. Might as well take advantage of the attractions."

Intrepidly, she dove onto his lap. "I say I'm sitting on the best attraction in town." She scattered smacking kisses all over his face. "How about it, sweetness? If I let you take advantage of me, will you return the favor?"

"Gar-net, stop ravishing me," he said, dodging her wayward mouth. "I'm trying to show a little gallantry here. The least you can do is cooperate."

"Do you really, really want to go out?"

"No. But if we don't, you'll think the only reason I made this trip was to take you to bed."

"And you don't want to do that?"

"God, yes, I want to do that. Can't you tell?"

She wiggled her bottom. "I can tell." Attacking his shirt buttons, she nuzzled his chest as she worked her way downward. "A compromise, then. First we'll have a reunion. After that, if you still insist, we'll do the town."

"You are a very persuasive woman, Garnet Brindisi."

"I take it that means yes."

"Yes, that's what it means."

"Oh, goody. Right before you knocked, I was having this great fantasy." She whispered the details in his ear.

"You want to try that here?"

"Well, there are only three steps and you don't have a Rhett Butler mustache, but I expect my imagination can fill in the missing parts."

In one swiftly coordinated movement, Gray stood with her cradled against his chest and strode through the bedroom door.

The reunion was unforgettable, and not once did Garnet need to rely on her imagination.

Ten

"What's your pleasure?"

Gray's knife halted in the middle of slicing his prime rib. He cast a surreptitious glance around and resumed cutting, seemingly satisfied that none of the nearby diners had overheard. Then he treated her to one of those bone-melting quarter smiles. "You took care of that quite exhaustively not very long ago."

She leaned close, her mouth beside his ear. "I couldn't help myself. Being carried off to bed punched all the right buttons. I never dreamed I'd find a man big and strong enough to pick me up that way."

"Stop pandering to my ego. You're not very heavy."

"But there is a lot of me, and you know exactly what to do with every bit of it."

"I was right the first time. You are a shameless flirt." He tested his Yorkshire pudding. "Now, finish your dinner. We have a long night ahead of us."

"You better believe it," she said, squeezing his arm and giving him a saucy wink. "That's why I ordered this lobster ravioli. Everybody knows pasta's a better source of energy than that slab of red meat you're gnawing on."

"You just love taunting me, don't you?"

"Nope, I just love you."

Garnet hadn't meant for her question to send them

off on that particular tangent. But sexy talk was a natural extension of the sensual harmony that linked them. She had been inquiring whether he preferred to take in a lounge show or wander through the casino. They decided to do a little of both, so she undertook his instruction in the fine art of video poker.

As they approached the cage to exchange some bills, she said, "Your first move should always be to set a limit. In other words, how much money are you willing to lose tonight?"

Gray lifted his shoulders, not looking too thrilled at the prospect of losing any. "A hundred bucks, I guess."

"Fair enough. Play your cards right, sweet stuff, and I'll double your investment in an hour." Armed with ten rolls of quarters, she led him up and down an aisle of electronic machines, checking the payoff table and the payout schedule posted on the front of each. "Most of these are 'jacks or better,' which means if your final hand has a pair of jacks or higher, you'll win something."

"How reassuring."

"Don't be such a pessimist. You have me looking out for your best interests." She halted in front of a machine about midway down the aisle. "This is the one for us."

"What makes it different from the rest?"

"It feels right."

"*Feels* right?" He whacked a roll of quarters on the change tray. "How can you predict results based on such unscientific selection criteria?"

"What do I need with scientific selection criteria when I have gambler's instincts? Now pay attention.

Most machines give better odds and better payoffs when you play maximum coin."

"What's that mean?"

"If you want to limit your risk to about a dollar per game, stay away from a dollar machine. Pick a quarter one, and feed it five coins each time. The jackpot on ours is five grand. Give it a try."

Gray deposited five quarters. "Okay, coach, now what?"

"Push the 'Deal' button."

They stood there playing for half an hour, him dealing, her advising, winning and losing until his hundred dollars had dwindled to thirty. "Maybe I ought to quit before I lose it all," he suggested.

"Are you joking? There's a royal flush coming up in the next five minutes. Count on it."

He continued to ply the machine with quarters, and sure enough, lights, bells, and whistles started going off. Coins jingled as they poured out of the machine, and nearby players stopped to applaud a fellow traveler who had beaten the system.

"What did I do?" he asked, confused by all the furor.

"I'm sure to a hotshot basketball star this is pocket change, but you just won five thousand dollars, good lookin'."

His eyes widened. "Five *thousand*?"

"Yep. Here comes a nice lady who will prove it."

Once all the excitement had subsided and they were sauntering down a carpeted corridor to the late lounge show, Gray said, "I still don't believe it. You told me there was a royal flush in the cards, but I didn't equate it with so much money."

"Easy to see how the exhilaration gets in some people's blood, huh?"

"Yeah, I suppose so. It is kind of exciting." His hand unconsciously tapped the pocket of his double-breasted jacket where he'd put the casino check. After they were seated at a small table and had ordered drinks, he said, "I'll keep my hundred. The rest is yours."

"No, Gray. The rules are, winner takes all."

"Rules have not applied since the night I met you." He spread his hands on the glossy wood surface. "You came to Vegas to make as much as you could. I'm only here because you are, and I wouldn't have won it without you. Seems to me you've earned it."

"That's very generous, but I can't take money from you. It wouldn't be right."

"Why is it acceptable to take money from Mr. Whitt and his pals or from complete strangers, but not from me?"

"If you have to ask that, I doubt that you'd understand my explanation anyway." While he stared into his brandy, Garnet stared at the attractive, well-dressed blonde at the bar who was checking out Gray.

"You think accepting this money from me would be akin to getting paid for sexual favors?"

She looked back at him and smiled. "Pretty insightful for a man. I'd say it's a little more complicated than that, but yes, basically I would feel you were giving it to me because we're involved."

"That's crazy," he said indignantly. "How did you come up with an irrational idea like that?"

"It's just the way I feel, okay?" The blonde still

had her predatory gaze trained on Gray, and it was starting to annoy Garnet. "Look, if you're hell-bent on giving the money away, donate it to the Rodeo scholarship fund."

He shook his head, clearly frustrated. "Boy, did I have it pegged right when I called you a paradox. You're a fanatic about the college fund, yet willing to turn down a substantial donation to it."

"Maybe I'm just being unpredictable to keep you on your toes." She took a sip of her champagne cocktail, making eye contact with him over the flute's rim. "Don't they say predictability leads to boredom? I'd hate to bore you."

She loved the way his eyes darkened, loved knowing she had the power to communicate her thoughts without words. "There's not a chance in hell you'd ever bore me." He pushed back his cuff to see the time. "Although suddenly the idea of bed does sound appealing. If you've had your fill of downstairs fun, I'm ready . . . to go up."

"I think I'm already halfway there," she said, patting her heart, which had gone wild. "But first I have a tiny bit of business. Will you excuse me for a minute?"

Garnet could feel his gaze following her as she walked to the bar and gave the woman on the stool a few succinct tips. Then, satisfied she'd made her point, she returned to Gray and picked up her evening bag.

"Do you know her?"

"I do now. That, my gallant knight, is a member of the world's oldest profession. She was trolling in my territorial waters and I had to fire a warning shot across her bow."

Shock registered on his face. "I hadn't once looked her way. How could you tell?"

"Call it woman's instinct." She took his arm in a possessive hold and, with a smug smile, deliberately paraded past the blonde.

"You really are a show-off sometimes," he said as soon as the elevator door closed.

She crowded close, ran her hand over his tie, and tugged on his belt. "Uh-huh. And boy, do I have a show planned for you tonight."

Very early Sunday morning Garnet slid from beneath the covers, taking pains not to wake Gray. He'd maintained such a grueling pace the past couple of weeks, he needed every minute of sleep he could get. She had tried to impress that upon him last night, but he hadn't been very receptive.

What he had been was insatiable. Her body felt warm and tingly in the aftermath of pleasure. She carefully closed the bathroom door and turned on the shower. She had awakened at three with a vision or inspiration, something telling her to go back to the video poker machines, that she too could win a jackpot. Anyone other than a diehard gambler would scoff, but Garnet knew better than to ignore such signs.

She showered quickly and dashed on a little eye makeup and lipstick. At this time on a Sunday morning the casino crowd would be sparse. Besides, the only person she cared about impressing was Gray. While she was pulling on violet slacks and a fluffy white sweater, she smiled at his sleeping form. When she got back with her own jackpot, she was going to wake him in a shower of bills.

Garnet checked her cash stash, debating whether to take the whole amount or leave some behind. Of course, she wouldn't feed it all to the machines, but having her winnings with her fed her confidence that she could increase them. She found the key in Gray's trouser pocket and silently let herself out the door.

It was shaping up as another lucky day.

Gray heard a distant commotion and stirred, unsure where the racket was coming from. He had slept deeply for the first time in several weeks and was having trouble shaking off the grogginess. He reached for Garnet, found her missing, and that brought him more fully awake. "Garnet?" No answer.

He forced himself to get up and shuffle over to look into the suite's parlor. Empty. But the noise was clearer now, urgent, muffled voices and scuffling sounds right outside in the hall.

When he heard the scream, he went icy all over. "Garnet!" He sprinted for the door and wrenched it open. Then the ice turned to fire. Her attacker had a knife and Garnet was on the floor, rolling, kicking, fighting to fend off the slashing blade. There was blood on her white sweater.

Fury whipped through him like a bolt of lightning. Gray pounced on the man from behind and slammed him against a wall. He went for the wrist first, heard a bone snap, kicked at the knife as it fell, and used his foot to send it skittering out of reach.

Doubling up both fists, he gave vent to his rage with a hail of punishing body blows. The man struggled briefly, but he soon sank to the floor, no match for Gray's size and strength, or for the magnitude of his violent reaction.

Immobilizing his victim with a knee to the kidneys, he turned to Garnet, who was sitting with her back against a wall. "Are you all right?"

Wide-eyed, her mouth open, she nodded. Her breathing was as choppy as his.

"Are you sure? The blood . . ."

Dazed, she held her arms out and examined the red-welling gashes. "Just surface cuts, I think. He was trying to intimidate me rather than do me in." Glaring at the inert mugger, she said, "He's not much bigger than I am. I thought I could handle him."

Gray gave a vile one-word assessment of her judgment, then said through gritted teeth, "Get inside."

"But—"

"Garnet, go into the room and call security, unless you want me to carve this creep up in pieces with his own knife." He was barely hanging onto the shreds of his temper. The itch to teach the punk a painful lesson was getting stronger by the second.

She got slowly to her feet and went to do his bidding. Too bad she hadn't been more obedient when he'd warned her about coming here. Seconds later she appeared again, carrying a large bath towel, which she extended to him.

"In the interest of modesty, you might want to wrap this around yourself."

Gray looked down, horrified. He'd just had a fist fight in the hallway of a major hotel, naked as the day he was born. Wouldn't that make great newspaper copy? "Hell and damnation, Garnet."

A swarm of security officers arrived pronto, armed to the teeth. Dour-faced, they were not pleased that an incident like this had happened on their turf. With so much money floating around at all times, security was a primary concern of every casino.

Garnet watched as Gray assumed command. Six feet six made an imposing statement, even clad in a pink towel. "First thing I'd advise is you get that sleaze out of my sight. I might change my mind about finishing him off."

A pair of security personnel carted the assailant off. Then Gray asked, "Any of you trained as paramedics? Miss Brindisi has lost some blood."

All of a sudden she was being fawned over like a princess. Taken to the couch, her wounds cleansed and treated, assured that while they didn't believe she'd suffered serious injuries, they would certainly summon an ambulance. "Hey, guys, relax. My hide is Texas tough. It'll take more than that wimpy pig-sticker to do real damage to me."

Gray left, but just long enough to throw on a pair of navy cords and a fisherman's sweater. His feet stayed as bare as the rest of him had been only minutes ago. He stationed himself at the door to listen while she gave her account of the episode to the remaining officers.

"I went down to the casino floor about seven. There weren't many people around at that time. I'd only been there a little while when this man, the one who followed me, began playing video poker a couple of machines away from me. As you saw, he was well dressed, pleasant looking, and we sort of started commiserating with each other. You know, one loser to another."

Gray muttered something under his breath and began stalking the room. "Anyway, to make a long story short, I later won a two-thousand-dollar jackpot and decided to come back up here and share my good fortune . . . with Mr. Kincaid."

He halted a second, then resumed his prowling. "I got an uneasy feeling when the same man turned up on my elevator, but again, he smiled and joked as if we were old buddies. It wasn't until he followed me out, crowding real close behind, that I knew something was wrong. By the time he grabbed me around the neck, I was prepared to fight. The rest is pretty much what you saw."

Gray threw up his hands and looked to the ceiling, as if invoking a higher authority to intervene. After a few more questions the security people stood to leave. Gray trailed them to the door and stepped outside. All she could hear were muted voices. When he came back to the parlor, Garnet could see that the real inquisition was yet to come. He continued to roam aimlessly, his restless activity so alien, she could only look on in amazement.

"Don't you remember me telling you to watch out for questionable characters if you insisted on coming here?"

"I remember. But how could I know that—"

"And why the hell did you sneak out of here at dawn? Didn't it enter your mind that it would be nice to wake up together for a change? We don't get many chances."

Gray cursing, pacing, practically shouting, didn't compute. Her first instinct was to placate him. "There's nothing I wanted to do more than stay with you. But you're so tired, have been under such a strain lately, that I wanted you to sleep as much as possible. You know how unlikely that is if we're in bed for any length of time."

That curbed his wrath temporarily. "Yeah, I know. But haven't you noticed, making love is energizing, not tiring?"

"Yes," she murmured, delighted that he shared her feeling about lovemaking and would be open enough to say so. "Still, I thought sleep was the best option for you."

"It's a good thing I wasn't sleeping too soundly. Otherwise you might be in the hospital or the morgue about now."

"Yes." It had begun to sink in precisely how dangerous a situation she'd been in, and her shakiness was increasing instead of ebbing. "I'm very relieved that you were here to rescue me."

"*Relieved!* Garnet, that was no goddamn tea party out there. I went crazy, used my fists, could easily have kept pounding that guy until I killed him."

"You probably just reacted rather than thinking."

He ran both hands through his hair, a nervous gesture she'd never seen before. "You don't know how careful I have been about avoiding fights. I've always been bigger than most everyone around me, and it would be easy for someone my size to use that advantage. So I've always taken care to go the other way, to steer clear of violence. But today I went berserk. There's no other way to describe it."

Garnet sprang from the couch and went to put her hand on his shoulder. "I'm sorry you were put in that position because of me."

"I could overlook all the other lapses, but the dumbest stunt of all was presuming you could best a criminal who was holding a knife at your throat." Gray clamped his hands on her upper arms and shook her. "He might have *killed* you, lady," he roared, "just because you didn't have sense enough to hand over the friggin' money."

"Four thousand dollars is a lot, can do a lot. There's no way I was going to hand over that much to some two-bit hood. Not while I have breath left in me."

"You're crazy, and what's worse, you make me crazy." He shook her once more, then looked at his hands and stomped away, as if he feared his anger would again take control.

He went to the window and she could almost see him talking to himself, striving for the composure that was inherent to him. He had a very strong will, and when he spoke again, his voice had its usual cool detachment. "From the first moment I laid eyes on you, I knew you'd be trouble. Today confirms that first impressions are usually reliable. Garnet, I don't have time for this kind of grief."

"That does it! I've heard enough of your accusations! You're acting like *I* committed a crime." She'd gone through a traumatic, potentially life-threatening experience, and the fight-or-flight rush had diminished, leaving her weak and slightly nauseous. She needed to be held, comforted, but

Gray was crashing around like a storm trooper, reading her the riot act.

It wasn't fair. After all the unconditional support she'd given him and the patience she had shown, he had the nerve to yell at her, to shake her. She was seething, about to explode.

"You're just like everyone else in my life, never there for me, concerned only with yourself, what you want, and what's good for you." *Grammy took time to care, but I no longer have her.* "My parents stayed so absorbed with each other, they barely knew I existed. Ty's got his ranch and nothing else matters to him. 'Aw, don't worry about Garnet. She's strong and resilient, she'll manage.' That's what they all say."

She thrust her chin out, proud and defiant. "And I can too. I was doing fine before you, I can get along without you once you're gone. I'm so much trouble, you should pack your bag and head for the door."

"Garnet," he said, approaching her, looking calm and apparently bent on reasoning. Hurt, angry, and shaking almost uncontrollably, she was beyond reason.

"No, you've said enough. I mean it. Get your stuff together and get out." If he didn't, she was going to dissolve in a bawling fit, which she simply would not do in front of him.

He looked at his watch and swore. "If I don't catch that plane, I won't make it to San Diego for the game."

"Go! That's the most important thing to you anyway."

"I'll call you when we both get back to Houston."

"Don't bother. I'm sure it would be too much trouble."

As soon as he went into the bedroom, Garnet escaped to the Whitts' suite. She had given Gray too much, and she couldn't bear watching him walk out of her life and take it all with him.

He had flat-out blown it. Gray stood on his balcony and gazed across the Southwest Freeway toward Garnet's house. So close . . .

Since his return to Houston almost a week ago, he had called her several times every day. She had refused to see him, wouldn't even listen long enough for him to explain why he'd turned on her after the attack. He hadn't understood himself, until he had boarded the plane and the adrenaline high crashed. Then the realization seized him like a sharp pain.

Fear. He'd been so scared that scum was going to kill her that he'd lost it completely. And because being totally out of control was foreign to him, he'd acted like an idiot, lashing out at Garnet instead of taking her in his arms and telling her how thankful he was that she hadn't been hurt.

He had realized something else on that short flight. Garnet was wrong if she thought the team was the most important thing in his life. It wasn't. She was. And first thing Monday morning he had told Bennett so, fully prepared to lose his job over it, and not caring.

Gray had spent so much time dwelling on their differences, convincing himself she wasn't the right type for him, he'd missed the fundamental point that he had already fallen in love with her. Boy, it sure was easy to screw things up when it came to the business of love.

Susannah should see him now, tied in knots and running in circles, driven solely by emotion. Willing to sacrifice everything he'd wanted and worked for simply because he loved a woman. He smiled grimly. So much for not being able to feel deeply.

Only trouble was, Garnet had no way of knowing about his transformation. From all indications, she didn't care. That left him no alternative except to devise an extravagant means of persuading the lady to give him a second chance. She was so warmhearted and generous, and she'd claimed to love him. With those three things in his favor, he told himself he couldn't fail.

But it took another week to set things up and by that time he had learned what it meant to be a bundle of nerves. His hands shook as he waited in his car around the corner from the Whitts' house. He'd had to enlist the couple's help to lure Garnet out into the open so he could stage his abduction.

When the lurid green convertible pulled into the Whitts' driveway, he drove up to block it. By the time she got the door open, he was standing by to capture her. God, it felt good just to hold her hand.

"Gray! What do you think you're doing?"

She tried to sound stern, but he could tell she was a little bit intrigued. "I'm kidnapping you for the night."

"You and what army?"

He held her fingers tightly when she started to pull away. "Just me. And it'll be simpler for both of us if you come along with no complaints, no questions." When she opened her mouth to protest again, he touched her shoulder. "Please, Garnet. I really need to talk to you."

He sensed her yielding seconds before she looked into his eyes, then nodded. "I suppose I owe you that much."

"No, it's the other way around. I'm the one who owes you—a big apology and an explanation that makes sense." He guided her toward his car and solicitously tucked her in the passenger seat.

"Oh, goody. I've always liked a man who recognizes the value of groveling."

Gray grinned and started the car, willing to indulge her smart mouth. "Going to make me pay, huh?" Once she learned his intentions, he hoped it wouldn't be necessary to grovel.

"Kidnapping is a federal offense. Any reason I should let you off easy?"

"Maybe. We'll see." He pulled onto Bellaire going toward the Loop. "You forced my hand by refusing to see me. Didn't you know I wouldn't give up?"

"No, actually I didn't." He scowled at her and she shrugged. "Oh, I assumed you'd want to do the polite, gentlemanly thing and apologize. Beyond that, I figured you'd be happy to say good riddance."

"Surely you know better than that."

"Why? It isn't as though you've invested a lot of time or gotten intensely involved with me."

She was goading him again and his temper flared. Now that he'd let go, he seemed doomed to be at the mercy of his emotions. "Lady, you don't have a clue."

She challenged him with an arched brow and silence.

"I took the rap once for being a cold fish, and I deserved it. But not this time. I *am* involved with you, Garnet Brindisi. So thoroughly that sometimes I feel like I'm going to come unglued from the force of it. Is that *intense* enough for you?"

Her eyes registered surprise, then curiosity. "What are you saying?"

"You strike me as a logical thinker. See if you can figure it out for yourself."

She grinned, signaling Gray that she'd recognized her own taunt from their first meeting. "Suppose I'm not as logical as you. Suppose you spell it out more clearly."

"Last Monday I stormed into Bennett Townsend's office and issued an ultimatum. He could either get off my case and start treating you with respect or I was out the door."

"You said that? Did you mean it?"

He blew out an exasperated sigh. "Garnet, there's one thing you can take to the bank. If I say something, you can bet I mean it."

She half turned in the seat, animation returning, acting more like the woman he loved. "What did he do?"

"Like most bullies, he backed down. Said he wanted me to stay on, even apologized, after a fashion."

"So conditions are better with your job? That must be a relief."

"Yes. But it could be temporary. Rumors are flying

thick and fast that the Wildcatters are definitely going to be sold this time, and soon. Which means I'll probably get my walking papers right behind Bennett."

Her lips twitched in a kind of sly little smile that suggested she knew a secret. "Don't pack your bags yet. I'm sure the new owners will want you to stay exactly where you are."

"More of your gambler's intuition?"

The smile spread. "Something like that." They rode a ways without speaking. As Gray negotiated the interchange onto the North Freeway, he kept glancing at Garnet, who was chewing on her lip. At last she looked at him. "If we're to go any further with a relationship, the issue of my poker playing has to be resolved. We can't keep replaying that scene in Vegas."

"I know." Gray had examined his irrational objection to her gambling from every angle. "I used up a lot of the past two weeks thinking about that and I'm not sure if what I've come up with will sound plausible to you."

"Try me."

"I'd never met anybody like you, yet you just took me by storm. That was nearly impossible for me to deal with. I kept searching for something, anything, to make you less appealing, so I latched on to the gambling."

"I'm truly not addicted, Gray. It doesn't rule my life." She wet her lips, studied her intertwined fingers. "If there were absolutely no alternative, I could give it up."

"I will never ask you to do that, Garnet," he promised solemnly. "And I will never make an issue of it again. I'm done with fighting my feelings because I can finally admit I want you just the way you are."

"Thank you," she whispered, her eyes misty. "That means a lot, coming from you." She looked up and saw he had taken the Holzwarth exit. "Are we going where I think we're going?"

"Yeah." The silver-skinned blimp was visible now, tethered by the nose cone, but bobbing gently in the gathering dusk. He'd called ahead and been told weather conditions were ideal for flying. "They're expecting us."

"They are?"

"You sound doubtful."

"It's just that I've been trying for years to get a ride, and have never been able to come close." She eyed him suspiciously. "I suppose because you're a high-powered man about town all you had to do was pick up the phone."

He stopped the car at the edge of the pavement and walked around to collect her. "It took a bit more effort than a phone call. But I wanted to impress you and I can be pretty persistent when it comes to getting what I want."

"Well." She was trying not to weaken, trying and failing. A smile got the best of her and she sighed. "All right, I'm impressed."

They crossed the wide grassy expanse to where the crew stood waiting. After a guided tour around the exterior, they climbed a narrow set of fold-down steps to reach the passenger compartment. "Oh," she exclaimed. "I thought it would be much larger."

"Room for only six, plus me," the pilot explained, sitting down to take the controls.

Garnet and Gray claimed a pair of the wooden chairs that were bolted to the floor, and the captain began supplying them with a running commentary of statistics about the blimp. Soon they were airborne and cruising above the city. "Thirty miles an hour won't get you anywhere in a hurry," the pilot commented.

"But what a ride," Garnet said. "This is great." Eyes gleaming with excitement, she grabbed one of Gray's hands, using the other to point out familiar landmarks.

When it had turned completely dark, the electronics technician on board told them about the night sign called "Super Skytacular." Covering more than a hundred feet along the blimp's side, with over seven thousand lights, it flashed messages that were visible to those on the ground. He demonstrated with a public service announcement supporting recycling.

Garnet clapped her hands together like a happy child. "I can't believe this is actually happening." They watched another series of announcements. She turned to Gray. "Okay, I'm *really* impressed."

"Watch the next one," he said, aware of a tightening in his stomach. A cow bounced across the screen, chased by a horse with a rope-twirling cowboy astride it.

"The rodeo!" She bent over to examine the screen more closely, but it went dark, then blinked back on with a series of basketball plays. "This is so clever. How do they do it?"

"Computer with a mouse," the technician answered.

Next came a multitiered wedding cake, which

brought a tiny frown to Garnet's face. But that was nothing compared to the shock of the message that followed.

GARNET BRINDISI, WILL YOU MARRY ME?

She froze, speechless, which was a rare occurrence. Gaping at Gray, she shook her head. In disbelief, he hoped, not refusal.

"I asked you once, but that was when you didn't think honor was a good enough reason for marriage."

"I haven't changed my mind."

"What if I have? What if I tell you I'm proposing for a very different reason?"

"*Are* you telling me that?"

"Yes. I want you to marry me because I love you and don't think there's any way I can live without you. Is that more what you had in mind when you refused the first proposal?"

Her eyes started to tear. "Well, dang. What a time to cry."

He smiled indulgently and blotted the moisture, happy for any chance to touch her. "Well, dang. Are you going to give me an answer, or what?"

Even tear-streaked, she was beautiful. "Sweet William, you're the love of my life. You know what the answer is. I was just waiting for you to do it right."

"Say it."

"First I'd better warn you that I won't be nearly as patient as your first fiancée. If you're expecting another two-year engagement, think again."

"I was thinking maybe two days. We could get married in Tahoe and you can introduce me to your parents at the same time."

"You, Gray Kincaid, are a very persuasive man."

"Then don't keep me in suspense any longer. Give me your answer before I self-destruct."

"Yes, yes, yes! I'll marry you."

They watched the computerized lights blaze the message,

SHE SAID, "YES, YES, YES!"

Then with typical Garnet enthusiasm, she wrapped herself around him. "This is the most wonderful proposal ever, Gray. It's perfect. I love you for thinking of it. No, I love you, period."

When he said, "And I love you, because you're you," she melted against him. His heart seemed to swell with joy and hope and a million other possibilities. Gray knew it would always be this way.

She had that effect on him.

THE EDITOR'S CORNER

Come join the celebration next month when LOVE-
SWEPT reaches its tenth anniversary! When the line
was started, we made a very important change in the
way romance was being published. At the time, most
romance authors published under a pseudonym, but
we were so proud of our authors that we wanted to
give them the credit and personal recognition they
deserved. Since then LOVESWEPT authors have
always written under their own names and their pic-
tures appear on the inside covers of the books.

Right from the beginning LOVESWEPT was at the cutting edge, and as our readership changes, we change
with them. In the process, we have nurtured writing
stars, not only for romance, but for the publishing
industry as a whole. We're proud of LOVESWEPT
and the authors whose words we have brought to
countless readers over the last ten years.

The lineup next month is indeed something to
be proud about, with romances from five authors
who have been steady—and stellar—contributors to
LOVESWEPT since the very beginning and one up-
and-coming name. Further, each of these six books
carries a special anniversary message from the author
to you. So don't let the good times pass you by. Pick
up all six books, then sit back and enjoy!

The first of these treasures is **WILDFIRE**, LOVE-
SWEPT #618 by Billie Green. Nobody can set aflame

a woman's passion like Tanner West. He's spent his life breaking the rules—and more than a few hearts—and makes being bad seem awfully good. Though small-town Texas lawyer Rae Anderson wants a man who'd care for her and give her children, she finds herself rising to Tanner's challenge to walk on the wild side. This breathtaking romance is just what you've come to expect from super-talented Billie!

Kay Hooper continues her *Men of Mysteries Past* series with **THE TROUBLE WITH JARED**, LOVESWEPT #619. Years before, Jared Chavalier had been obsessed by Danica Gray, but her career as a gemologist had driven them apart. Now she arrives in San Francisco to work on the Mysteries Past exhibit of jewelry and discovers Jared there. And with a dangerous thief afoot, Jared must risk all to protect the only woman he's ever loved. Kay pulls out all the stops with this utterly stunning love story.

WHAT EMILY WANTS, LOVESWEPT #620 by Fayrene Preston, shocks even Emily Stanton herself, but she accepts Jay Barrett's bargain—ten days of her company for the money she so desperately needs. The arrangement is supposed to be platonic, but Emily soon finds she'll do just about anything . . . except let herself fall in love with the man whose probing questions drive her into hiding the truth. Fayrene delivers an intensely emotional and riveting read with this different kind of romance.

'TIL WE MEET AGAIN, LOVESWEPT #621 by Helen Mittermeyer, brings Cole Whitford and Fidelia Peters together at a high school reunion years after she'd disappeared from his life. She's never told him the heartbreaking reason she'd left town, and once the silken web of memories ensnares them both, they have to decide whether to let the past divide them once more . . . or to admit to a love that time has made only more precious. Shimmering with heartfelt emotion, **'TIL WE MEET AGAIN** is Helen at her finest.

Romantic adventure has never been as spellbinding as **STAR-SPANGLED BRIDE**, LOVESWEPT #622 by Iris Johansen. When news station mogul Gabe Falkner is taken by terrorists, he doesn't expect anyone to come to his rescue, least of all a golden-haired angel. But photojournalist Ronnie Dalton would dare anything to set free the man who'd saved her from death years ago, the one man she's always adored, the only man she dares not love. Iris works her bestselling magic with this highly sensual romance.

Last is **THE DOCTOR TAKES A WIFE**, LOVESWEPT #623 by Kimberli Wagner. The doctor is Connor MacLeod, a giant of a Scot who pours all his emotions into his work, but whose heart doesn't come alive until he meets jockey Alix Benton. For the first time since the night her life was nearly ruined, Alix doesn't fear a man's touch. Then suspicious accidents begin to happen, and Connor must face the greatest danger to become Alix's hero. Kimberli brings her special touch of humor and sizzling desire to this terrific romance.

On sale this month from Bantam are four spectacular women's fiction novels. From *New York Times* bestselling author Amanda Quick comes **DANGEROUS**, a breathtaking tale of an impetuous miss— and a passion that leads to peril. Boldness draws Prudence Merryweather into one dangerous episode after another, while the notorious Earl of Angelstone finds himself torn between a raging hunger to possess her and a driving need to keep her safe.

Patricia Potter's new novel, **RENEGADE**, proves that she is a master storyteller of historical romance. Set during the tumultuous days right after the Civil War, **RENEGADE** is the passionate tale of Rhys Redding, the Welsh adventurer who first appeared in **LIGHT-NING** and Susannah Fallon, who must trust Rhys with her life while on a journey through the lawless South.

Pamela Simpson follows the success of **FORTUNE'S CHILD** with the contemporary novel **MIRROR, MIRROR**. When an unexpected inheritance entangles Alexandra Wyatt with a powerful family, Allie finds herself falling in love. And as she succumbs to Rafe Sloan's seductive power, she comes to suspect that he knows something of the murder she'd witnessed as a child.

In a dazzling debut, Geralyn Dawson delivers **THE TEXAN'S BRIDE**, the second book in Bantam's series of ONCE UPON A TIME romances. Katie Starr knows the rugged Texan is trouble the moment he steps into her father's inn, yet even as Branch is teasing his way into the lonely young widow's heart, Katie fears her secret would surely drive him away from her.

Also on sale this month in the Doubleday hardcover edition is **MOONLIGHT, MADNESS, AND MAGIC**, an anthology of original novellas by Suzanne Forster, Charlotte Hughes, and Olivia Rupprecht, in which a journal and a golden locket hold the secret to breaking an ancient family curse.

Happy reading!

With warmest wishes,

Nita Taublib

Nita Taublib
Associate Publisher

OFFICIAL RULES TO WINNERS CLASSIC SWEEPSTAKES

No Purchase necessary. To enter the sweepstakes follow instructions found elsewhere in this offer. You can also enter the sweepstakes by hand printing your name, address, city, state and zip code on a 3" x 5" piece of paper and mailing it to: Winners Classic Sweepstakes, P.O. Box 785, Gibbstown, NJ 08027. Mail each entry separately. Sweepstakes begins 12/1/91. Entries must be received by 6/1/93. Some presentations of this sweepstakes may feature a deadline for the Early Bird prize. If the offer you receive does, then to be eligible for the Early Bird prize your entry must be received according to the Early Bird date specified. Not responsible for lost, late, damaged, misdirected, illegible or postage due mail. Mechanically reproduced entries are not eligible. All entries become property of the sponsor and will not be returned.

Prize Selection/Validations: Winners will be selected in random drawings on or about 7/30/93, by VENTURA ASSOCIATES, INC., an independent judging organization whose decisions are final. Odds of winning are determined by total number of entries received. Circulation of this sweepstakes is estimated not to exceed 200 million. Entrants need not be present to win. All prizes are guaranteed to be awarded and delivered to winners. Winners will be notified by mail and may be required to complete an affidavit of eligibility and release of liability which must be returned within 14 days of date of notification or alternate winners will be selected. Any guest of a trip winner will also be required to execute a release of liability. Any prize notification letter or any prize returned to a participating sponsor, Bantam Doubleday Dell Publishing Group, Inc., its participating divisions or subsidiaries, or VENTURA ASSOCIATES, INC. as undeliverable will be awarded to an alternate winner. Prizes are not transferable. No multiple prize winners except as may be necessary due to unavailability, in which case a prize of equal or greater value will be awarded. Prizes will be awarded approximately 90 days after the drawing. All taxes, automobile license and registration fees, if applicable, are the sole responsibility of the winners. Entry constitutes permission (except where prohibited) to use winners' names and likenesses for publicity purposes without further or other compensation.

Participation: This sweepstakes is open to residents of the United States and Canada, except for the province of Quebec. This sweepstakes is sponsored by Bantam Doubleday Dell Publishing Group, Inc. (BDD), 666 Fifth Avenue, New York, NY 10103. Versions of this sweepstakes with different graphics will be offered in conjunction with various solicitations or promotions by different subsidiaries and divisions of BDD. Employees and their families of BDD, its division, subsidiaries, advertising agencies, and VENTURA ASSOCIATES, INC., are not eligible.

Canadian residents, in order to win, must first correctly answer a time limited arithmetical skill testing question. Void in Quebec and wherever prohibited or restricted by law. Subject to all federal, state, local and provincial laws and regulations.

Prizes: The following values for prizes are determined by the manufacturers' suggested retail prices or by what these items are currently known to be selling for at the time this offer was published. Approximate retail values include handling and delivery of prizes. Estimated maximum retail value of prizes: 1 Grand Prize ($27,500 if merchandise or $25,000 Cash); 1 First Prize ($3,000); 5 Second Prizes ($400 each); 35 Third Prizes ($100 each); 1,000 Fourth Prizes ($9.00 each) ; 1 Early Bird Prize ($5,000); Total approximate maximum retail value is $50,000. Winners will have the option of selecting any prize offered at level won. Automobile winner must have a valid driver's license at the time the car is awarded. Trips are subject to space and departure availability. Certain black-out dates may apply. Travel must be completed within one year from the time the prize is awarded. Minors must be accompanied by an adult. Prizes won by minors will be awarded in the name of parent or legal guardian.

For a list of Major Prize Winners (available after 7/30/93): send a self-addressed, stamped envelope entirely separate from your entry to: Winners Classic Sweepstakes Winners, P.O. Box 825, Gibbstown, NJ 08027. Requests must be received by 6/1/93. DO NOT SEND ANY OTHER CORRESPONDENCE TO THIS P.O. BOX.

SWP 9/92